THE CALL OF LEMNOS

THE CALL
OF LEMNOS

A SCIENCE FICTION NOVEL
LEMNOS, BOOK TWO

FRANCIS JARMAN

THE BORGO PRESS
MMXIII

THE CALL OF LEMNOS

Published by Wildside Press LLC

www.wildsidebooks.com

DEDICATION

For Felix

CONTENTS

"There are more things in heaven and earth, Horatio,
Than are dreamt of in your philosophy"

William Shakespeare, *Hamlet*

PROLOGUE
THE LAST WILL AND TESTAMENT OF GUARDIAN GRADE I (INTERMEDIATE LEVEL) MILLIYA JAHANGIRI

Authorization: The activation lock may be released one day after full proof of my death, or one year after formal registration of my disappearance. I'm not aiming to die, but you never know. This is just in case.

THERE ISN'T A GREAT DEAL for me to pass on to anyone, just some furniture, some clothes, some electronic toys, and what's left of my savings (not much). It all goes to my sister, Jeine Jahangiri, along with my sincere hope that she stops bitching at her husband. Let him be, Jeine, he's a good man, better than you deserve (some people would say). Anyway, sweetheart, you know what I mean.

The man that *I* love, John Burk, doesn't get anything, because if I'm dead any time soon he'll be dead too. In case that happens, I want people to know how brave he was, and how I dragged him into it. He's an idiot, but if he hadn't been I wouldn't have fallen in love with him. I don't want him to be forgotten.

You might well think that *I'm* the stupid one: a Guardian with a great career ahead of her who fell for an AdPop, a useless "drone" with a more than useless degree in Media Studies and a dead end job. To make it worse, I was already in a relationship (of sorts) when I met him, with a high-ranking Guardian, Rebek'a, not so much a woman, more a force of nature! It was no coincidence when we all found ourselves on the *Starstretcher*, speeding off from Terra in slide hyperdrive. And where were we going? To Lemnos, the only other planet in the universe known to have higher life forms.

Rebek'a screwed me (and I don't just mean literally), I realize that now. She was playing some pretty dangerous power games. She had friends in high places, on the Imperial Advisory Council, and they had an agenda. It must have been convenient that I was there in her life, hero-worshiping her, believing every word that she said.

I certainly believed her when she told me that the settlers on Lemnos were destroying the life forms there, including the mysterious *sqot*. The Government (which, as we all know, is *not* best friends with the Council) was encouraging them, she said. Someone low-profile—and not a Guardian—had to be sent out to Lemnos to investigate, someone with media skills, someone who could document the abuses and spread reports when he got back to Terra. A dangerous job, and someone expendable was needed, so—*he*. Those reports would incriminate the Government. Burk was the sort of man that she needed, and I was asked to recruit him: first to my bed, and then to the small matter of bringing down the Government of the Terran Empire.

"Fuck him as much as you like, princess"—those were her very words—"after all, he's only AdPop rubbish, and that's what they're there for, aren't they?"

Why did I have to fall for him?

Getting him onto the *Starstretcher* was the easy part. Getting *myself* onto the *Starstretcher* was much harder: I had to kill a couple of people, not people that anyone would miss, though, and then take on a different identity, as "Guardian Jo-anna".

Somehow the Government got wind of the plan. And all of a sudden there was a high-powered security official on board, Guardian Sousanna, on her way to Lemnos to investigate the settlers herself. She was like a goddess, Burk said, wise and beautiful, but ice-cold. She was clever, too. Burk was framed, on a stupid charge of being a pedophile. What a joke! Naturally they couldn't prove it, but they could use it to keep him in custody aboard the ship and prevent him from disembarking.

Before we could release him, though, something awkward happened. Burk found out, from Guardian Adriyan, another Government agent, that it was *someone else* who was encouraging the settlers to destroy the *sqot*. The game turned nasty. Rebek'a tasered Adriyan to death, making it look like a suicide, and we found out that Rebek'a and her friends had no real interest in saving the *sqot*. So at short notice the plan was changed: I would now shadow Guardian Sousanna on Lemnos, and Burk would return to Terra to testify against the Government. If either of us faltered, Rebek'a said, oozing all her charm, the other would die.

Rebek'a had managed to smuggle some *sqot* onto the *Starstretcher*, and had been secretly eating the "green gunk", as she called it. Sadistically, she tried to force Burk to taste some: "Enjoy! It's like eating a kiss. Or a scream. Or both at the same time."

There was a fight. She should have crushed him easily, but in some strange way the *sqot* helped us to overcome her. That *sqot* is very weird stuff! We put Rebek'a's unconscious body in one of the waste bins, where she would wake up only after we'd disembarked on Lemnos and *she* was on her way back to Terra.

Happy ending, you might think? We tell Guardian Sousanna the whole story, Burk gets a medal and I get promotion? You would be wrong. On board the ship is an old Scribe, Jacoob, a former Ciaranite rebel. He tells us that the Government genuinely wants to prevent the *sqot* from being destroyed—but only in order to factory-farm it, and then use it as an addictive drug to keep the Terrans docile. Which sounds like the dream of every Government, doesn't it? Such a drug will soon be needed, he says. Mysterious aliens, vicious and ruthless, have begun to attack isolated planetary settlements and transporter ships. Massacres without survivors. Horrific mutilations. Disembowelings.

When word of these "Outsiders" reaches Terra, there will be panic.

Burk and I—now known as "Markko Mann" and "Guardian Jo-anna"—have agreed that we have no other choice than to take the shuttle down to the surface of Lemnos and find out the truth. Rebek'a and her friends will try to kill us. We know too much. The Government would also prefer us dead, for the same reason.

They may think we know too much; actually, we know too little. Burk wants to save the *sqot*. How noble of him! Having experienced its peculiar powers, I'm not quite so sure. *Sqot* could be the most dangerous enemy ever faced by the human race, more dangerous by far than Ciaranites or Outsiders. Saving it could be an enormous mistake. I haven't discussed this with Burk yet.

Burk is acting foolishly, but with great goodness of intent. I know that this is unorthodox, but under these circumstances I request that he be granted posthumous reclassification from AdPop to UsePop status, so that his mortal remains, if any should be recovered, are treated with respect and subjected to individual and not mass processing.

I apologize for the informality of this document, which was recorded under difficult conditions.

* * * * * * *

No witnesses were present, but the date and full details of the name, status and rank of the author are

encoded in the protocol. The document is authenti-
cated to Security Level 4 by electronic voiceprint.

CHAPTER ONE
PASSING THE GATE

"NEXT! MOVE, MOVE! Or do you want to go straight back to Terra?"

Long queues had formed in front of the checkpoints on the control vessel, and security staff from the Planetary Governorate were pushing the disembarking passengers through as fast as they dared. Everyone—the passengers with their luggage, the Guardians with their scanners—was sweating from the strain. The time window for the shuttles to transfer the incomings down to the surface of Lemnos was not generous. Missing it was unthinkable: the passengers would have to be shunted back onto the *Starstretcher*, and the transporter would then miss its departure time, or be obliged to take the Terrans back to Terra. Either way, the powers that be would be understandably displeased.

To make it worse, docking at the Gate of Lemnos had been an ordeal for all concerned. The control vessel hadn't been designed with super-modern people transporters of the Starreacher Class in mind. The two spacecraft had clung and juddered together, Burk thought, like two overweight animals that were doing their best but had never mated before.

The security, identity and customs checks at the Gate were generally no more than rudimentary. It was assumed that the necessary vetting and screening had all been done back on Terra, before embarkation. That would have suited Burk, waiting in line at one of the parallel checkpoints, just perfectly. Unfortunately, he seemed to have chosen the slowest line of all, and a Guardian who was both chatty and officious.

Her hand-held scanner declared him to be "Markko Mann, media technician, AdPop, Lower Executive Level, authorized for Lemnos, Medium Stay".

"Media technician? *At last* they send us one—we need someone like you here!"

Her words were surprisingly friendly, given her unattractive appearance. Though much older, she was as big and butch as Guardian Rebek'a, with the same muscular haunches and forearms, and the same bull-like neck, but whereas in the case of Guardian Rebek'a everything fitted together terrifyingly well, Guardian Georgeena looked more like a pompous, badly assembled doll. The effect was not improved by the excessive number of scanners, laser pens, tasers, electronic notepads and personal communicators with which she had adorned herself. This display of self-importance was undermined slightly by the single red slash on her uniform, the badge of a modest Grade I Guardian.

"Yes, that's what I was told: Lemnos needs me. I'm happy to be here!"

Burk had miscalculated: this was far too breezy. The

Guardian's piggy eyes narrowed.

"It's *Guardian* to you.... AdPop. Don't forget that!" Then, as an afterthought: "And that's a good question: why have they only sent us an *AdPop* technician? Aren't there any Guardian or UsePop technical specialists?" She wrinkled her bulbous nose. "And a *man*, for that matter!"

"Sorry, Guardian, no disrespect was intended." He paused. "I really don't know why they sent me, instead of a Guardian technical expert. But I'm here now, and I can't change strata, can I?"

Which was exactly the point, had Guardian Georgeena only realized it. Burk had a false identity. It hadn't been necessary to alter his standard identity chip. On the *Starstretcher* they had manipulated the scanners with a temporary program that would override his real identity. And during docking they had sent this proxy identity through the wire to the scanners at the Gate, so that when he was scanned the information that was actually on his chip was suppressed.

It was a temporary measure, but very effective. Unfortunately, many Guardian specialists had additional chip implants containing more sensitive and detailed information, implants that they themselves might not even know about. So better to leave "Markko Mann" as a lowly AdPop than risk the security Guardians *not* seeing on their scanners the chip information that they would normally have expected to be implanted in a Guardian specialist.

"Looks strange to me. I could check it in the system,

I suppose, except that we happen to have an ongoing mass hypertransmission from the *Starstretcher*. Maybe I should, though."

Burk knew that that was bullshit, and that she wouldn't dare risk interrupting the enormous data transfer that was currently underway between the *Starstretcher* and the Lemnian planetary information system. Not in a million light years she wouldn't. So what he said next was not quite the gamble it may have seemed.

"Perhaps I could do it for you, Guardian? I am a media technician, after all. If we tapped into just *one* of the transmission channels, the chances of total system crash would be very, very small...."

Her reaction was predictable: "No, we haven't got time. And don't try to tell me my job, AdPop!"

To compensate for this loss of face, however, Burk had to be humiliated in some other way. She pointed at the small case he was carrying. Someone else (probably Milliya) had packed it for him. It would hardly contain anything incriminating, he thought.

"Open it. Quickly. Speed is of the essence."

There were still a number of passengers behind Burk, as the other checkpoints had been working faster than Guardian Georgeena's. Trust him to end up at *her* station! Burk had seen Milliya go through in one of the parallel queues with no fuss and in barely more than seconds. No wonder Guardian Georgeena was still only a Grade I.

To his great surprise, he had also seen the Scribe

Jacoob. Good for him! So he had been lucky after all in the lottery for surface leave. Presumably he would be returning to Terra on a later flight, maybe on a goods freighter (every kind of ship needed Scribes). Would the little hunchback be looking for souvenirs of Lemnos for his grandchildren—colored dust, or a tiny Goro-nut if he could afford it—as he had said? Or would he be spending the precious time on the surface in a romantic tryst with Guardian Abi? The slab-faced Grade I apparently had a hold over the Scribe (ugly Guardians typically terrorized or blackmailed timid male AdPops into providing such favors). "Slabface" herself he *hadn't* seen, though she might have gone through ahead of him. Or perhaps she'd had no luck in the lottery.

"What's this?" Guardian Georgeena asked, delicately lifting up an unprepossessing item of male underwear. Her colleagues to left and right, and some of the passengers too, sniggered unpleasantly. "Is this what the fashionable AdPop man-about-town is wearing these days?"

Burk cursed inwardly. Why had Milliya packed *that* for him? Then he thought: no, she's a clever girl, that's *precisely* the kind of underwear that "media technician Markko Mann" would wear!

"Oh dear, and here are yet more items from the same designer. How *chic*...." Then her voice dropped. "What is this, though? Surely not a *book*?"

No no no. Milliya couldn't have been so stupid, surely? She had packed one of his precious books of poetry! She knew how much he loved them. But could anyone imagine "Markko Mann" wallowing in verse? Never! People had stopped writing poetry altogether by the middle of the twenty-first century, and in these modern times hardly anyone read it. "Markko" certainly wouldn't. If the Guardian now double-checked his identity, he was lost. Burk sensed how everyone around them had tensed up, how they were now paying close attention as if expecting something to *happen.*

Her lips pursed with disapproval, Guardian Georgeena opened the book in a way that suggested that she was handling the unnatural and unhygienic object against any personal inclination to do so, and strictly in the call of duty. She tilted it towards the light in order to read what was on the title-page: "*The Stones and Crystals of Lemnos: A Guide for the Beginner Collector.*"

Yes—that's just what "Markko Mann" would be reading!

"Mr. Mann"—and the respectful address resonated with sarcasm—"I find it difficult to believe that you have been overloading a slide hyperdrive people transporter, the most sensitive and expensive vehicle ever constructed"—she paused dramatically, holding up the book for everyone to see—"with *this*? With trivial recreational matter in bulk paper form! Information that, as every fool ought to know, is available for free to anyone who needs it on Globopedia? Do you realize what it must have *cost* to propel this useless object half way across the universe?" She paused for effect. "Stupidity is the most likely explanation. Or are you perchance a *book fetishist*?"

This was a cue for laughter—which duly came. Burk wasn't amused, but he was willing to endure any petty humiliation, even a full body search, provided that it got him through the checkpoint.

"Well, you see, I'm a collector...."

She threw the book back into the case.

"Yes, sure, of worthless pebbles, but not of *books*! I should confiscate that rubbish for the waste bin, but the damage has already been done, has it not? Also, there is no law against books—not as *yet*—though there should be. Make sure that you jettison all paper items before your return flight. And don't even *think* of taking back any crystals that weigh more than a couple of grams. Oh, and you might consider looking for a more adult hobby? Because—"

A loud siren sounded, making the metallic walls of the control vessel reverberate unpleasantly and interrupting Guardian Georgeena's homily.

"Very well, shut the case and go through. That's the last shuttle, and you're holding everyone up."

CHAPTER TWO
DOWN TO THE SURFACE

THE SHUTTLE CRAFT had not been built with passenger comfort in mind. There were functional-looking passenger bays each with four seating berths, fully equipped with belts and secure-bars, aligned in facing pairs. Beside each berth was a container for vomit. The shuttle transfer was clearly not for the faint-hearted.

Burk saw that both Milliya and the Scribe Jacoob would be on the shuttle with him, and studiously ignored them, but the little hunchback pushed him towards the most distant bay, made him sit down, and then shepherded Milliya over as well.

"Let's talk, we don't have long," he began, but then stopped as a fourth passenger, who introduced himself to them as the partner (or "consort") of a wealthy UsePop heiress, made himself comfortable in the remaining berth and began to strap himself in.

"Aylwin's the name! So you're a media technician, then? I was right behind you in the queue! That Guardian lady gave you a proper working over, didn't she?" Then, noticing Milliya's badge of rank: "Oh dear, no offence meant!"

"None taken."

His pasty face lit up.

"As charming as she is beautiful! And tough as well, no doubt! Yes, that lady was only doing her job, of course. And what would we do without our charming Guardians to keep the known universe safe? I mean, we boys need looking after, don't we? I feel that bit more secure every time my little lady slips in between the sheets with me. *Then* the night holds no terrors! Between your good selves and my modest self, my wife should really have been a Guardian, she's got a kick like a stun taser, but she was too busy making money and looking after *me*, bless her! Oh, no offence, Guardian, I'm sure that *you* don't go around kicking people, except bad boys who deserve it! Perhaps your AdPop friend here needs to be disciplined occasionally?"

"Not very often. He's a good lad on the whole." Milliya found their new acquaintance rather more amusing than Burk did.

Aylwin leered. "On the *hole*! Clever! That's a good one! And when he's naughty, a bit of kicking and beating is never out of place in the bedroom, I've always said. *Tough love*. The best sort. A media technician, eh? Say no more! Made any good films recently, Mr. Media Man?" And, winking salaciously: "I'm sure you know what I mean! You'll be greeted on Lemnos, as the expression goes, like the Blessed Messiah (whoever that was, I think I missed that particular lesson at school)."

Noticing that Jacoob was becoming increasingly irritated by the man's inanities, Burk tried to stem the flow and change the direction of the conversation: "Will there be different stops on the surface? At different settlements, perhaps?"

"I can see that *you've* not been here before! There's only one stop, just as there's only one proper settlement: Lemnos City. Or *Sin* City, as we call it."

"And everyone lives there?"

"No, there are lots of farms and estates, but you can drive out to them in a transportation buggy, they're easy to hire. The bigger estates are further away, but there are flights by surface shuttle. I have the timetables on my personal communicator, if you're interested. We have our own shuttle, of course. My wife—Keesha's her name—will be collecting me. Can we drop you off somewhere? Where are you planning to go?"

"I was thinking of trying to see the whole planet if possible, and not just Lemnos City, before I go back to Terra."

"The whole planet? What—Limbo-Limbo-Land as well? You must be joking!"

"Limbo-Limbo-Land?"

"The other side of the planet. It's completely empty! Just a few research stations, and miles and miles of *sqot*! Sinister place. No-one really lives there."

"That sounds interesting. Might meet some aliens!"

"More likely it's crawling with Outsiders." Aylwin shuddered. "They split you open and spread your entrails all around. That's what I've been told."

"But you haven't actually been there?"

"Not if you *paid* me!"

"Then maybe I can find somewhere else that's a bit off the beaten track, but not quite so dangerous. For a kind of adventure holiday. You'd probably have to take lots of rations with you, or can you live off the land? Lemnian bananas, eh? I've heard of them. Got any cooking tips?"

"Ah, well, it doesn't have to be bananas, young man. The local vegetation can be *quite interesting*, and I'm not talking about bananas or ferns. I could tell you a thing or two that would, er, expand your horizons...."

There were mechanical sounds indicating that the shuttle might soon be departing. Jacoob now took action, leaning forward and looking intently into Aylwin's eyes. "My nephew here will be staying with me."

"And where will that be?"

"At the Lemnian Quarantine Station for Incurable Diseases—"

"Oh!"

"—where I am spending my final years. I am only a second level patient, so I was allowed back to Terra for a family funeral."

Aylwin shifted himself energetically backwards into the berth. "Incurable diseases?"

"Yes, the growth that you see on my back. It's a malignant and painful fungal condition, quite unstoppable, but my nephew has agreed to nurse me for the short time that I have left."

"Is it...er...infectious?" Aylwin was now speaking very quietly.

"Normally, yes. Virulent, in fact, in some cases. But Markko is genetically protected. Only non-relatives can catch the infection."

"Oh. I see."

Jacoob coughed, spraying the contents of his throat in all directions.

"Sorry. Don't worry about *that*. That's just my syphilitic cough—perfectly treatable with neoantibiotics."

Aylwin unstrapped himself quickly and got up, announcing that he needed to check that his cases had been stowed properly. The shuttle was only half full: there were plenty of free berths. He would obviously not be coming back.

The vessel began to move.

"Listen," the Scribe began again, "the rough part is coming now, when the shuttle moves out of orbit. And landing will be no fun either. In between, though, we need to talk."

He looked at Milliya.

"If this man comes back, my lady, it's *your* turn to deal with him. He seems to like violence. Why don't you hit him with the vomit box?"

Aylwin didn't come back, though.

The "wonder of the universe", the "most beautiful spacescape in the galaxy" as Globopedia called it, was a distinct disappointment, at least as seen through the dingy portholes of the shuttle. The Green Planet was no longer green, but gray-brown. The famous light-effects, resulting from the interplay of Zora, the star of Lemnos, with the twin Kallipygian moons, Ogrob and Darnoc, and the rich vegetation of the planet's surface, were nowhere in evidence. Not that Burk, Milliya and Jacoob were looking.

"I won't be staying long on the surface, and you shouldn't be seen with me. Remember: I'm a 'Ciaranite'!"

"So you managed to win the lottery for surface leave after all?"

"No." Jacoob smiled grimly. "If you want something badly enough, there are usually other ways to get it."

That sounded rather sinister to Burk, but Milliya was not impressed.

"Then in all your wisdom please tell us," she said, "what to do next? The Government will soon be hunting for their escaped prisoner"—she made a gesture in the direction of Burk—"beg pardon, *detainee*, and they'll be hunting for me too when they discover that the real Guardian Jo-anna is a corpse, and that I'm someone quite different."

"True enough, my lady."

"We're landing on a strange planet, to be met by people who all think we're on the same side as they are. When Guardian Rebek'a wakes up, though, and climbs out of that waste bin on the *Starstretcher* where we left her, even if by then she's already speeding back to Terra, she'll find some way to contact her friends and tell them to kill us, surely?"

"No—not true."

"Why not?"

"Because an hour ago I made *certain arrangements*. The waste bins will be unloaded into space as soon as the *Starstretcher* starts moving."

It took a moment for Burk and Milliya to comprehend fully what he was saying.

"I know—it's against Galactic Navigational Law. Nor is it too good for anyone who might happen to be sleeping off a hangover, or, in this case, a mild tasering, in one of the bins. But it had to be done. I knew that *you* weren't capable of killing her, my lady. You were lovers. As for you, Mr. Burk: I don't mean to be unkind, but I doubt whether you'd be capable of killing *anybody*."

Milliya said nothing. Withdrawn into herself, she stared blankly out into space.

"So, you see, there will be no warning from Guardian Rebek'a. The people who will meet you are thuggish and degenerate, but they won't be a threat to you. Indeed, they've been asked to help you."

Burk could sense how upset Milliya was, but waited for her to speak. When she remained silent, he said, "We can't go to these people. We can't use these contacts. We know now that they're our enemies. That they've been primed to feed us lies and false information."

Instead of replying to Burk, Jacoob spoke to Milliya: "That woman would have sacrificed you at any moment that was convenient. I don't know whether she had any feelings for you. If *you* had feelings for *her*, then make sure that she didn't die in vain—use the time that her death has given you to undo her wickedness."

The lights of the settlement could now be seen below. Once again, the shuttle began to rock and vibrate as the pilot aligned it for the descent into Lemnos City.

"Mr. Burk, did no-one ever tell you that, in the game of war, the safest place to be is: close to your enemy? Especially if your enemy hasn't realized who you are. Listen to the lies that these people tell you; uncover the truth about the evil that has been done here; and find out the names of the perpetrators."

"Will our testimony be enough? Milliya's a renegade Guardian, and I'm just an AdPop. Shouldn't we try to collect evidence?"

"You still have your personal communicator, my lady, but don't use it, don't even switch it on, or the Government will trace you. The other ones may have such resources, too. But...if one of them *does* speak out really loud and clear, bragging about what they have done, naming names, it might be worth switching it on as a recorder for a few minutes. It would be a risk, though: if they manage to trace you, there'll soon be a drone or a snatch squad of Guardians knocking on your door."

Milliya finally spoke up. "I'll do it. *We'll* do it."

"Thank you. As for me: I don't exist. We don't know each other. I'll be gone soon. But we have friends on Lemnos—someone will be watching you, and somehow we'll get you back to Terra. Exactly *how* I don't know yet. Look after him, my lady, he's not as tough as you are, mentally or physically. Enjoy your stay on Lemnos, Mr. Mann: I hope you find some interesting crystals for your collection. Oh look, I believe we're landing." And he ignored them for the rest of the short trip.

If Lemnos City was indeed a place of sinfulness and debauchery, there was nothing about its spaceport to suggest that. Once again, the cliché that all spaceports look the same was emphatically confirmed. The materials and fittings were trapped in a late twentieth-century timewarp—the period when such designs became standardized—and what had once been intended to look "ultra-modern" now looked nostalgically "Olde Worlde" without being a whit more attractive.

Burk noticed that the numerous souvenir shops, selling crystals, colored sands, Goro-nuts and tasteless "artworks" made from these products, were just larger versions of the stalls on the control vessel. There were also incredibly expensive recreational gadgets on sale (though who buys things like that at a spaceport?). You could acquire items of clothing emblazoned with references to Lemnos. These would no doubt distinguish you among your friends back on Terra as an experienced space-traveler—or (since these items were readily obtainable from shops on Terra too) as a complete pillock. The "jokes" on the jerkins and tee shirts were excruciatingly vulgar: "He squatted on some sqot...and look what's happened to his Goro-nuts!" was a typical one.

And then there were the restaurants and snack-bars. Some of the restaurants provided upmarket meals based on the standard rations for Guardians and UsePops (AdPops were generously permitted to eat there as well, if any tables were free and if they could afford to). Burk noticed a restaurant run by the Delicio Corporation—DELICIO DELIGHTS—and made a mental note never to eat *there*. They might not serve the tablets, bars and concentrates that he had been fed on the *Starstretcher*, but the meals would be made from essentially the same processed stuff, though in "recon-stituted" form. The more grungy-looking snack-bars were presumably only for AdPops.

More interesting were the restaurants serving typical Lemnian fare: dishes based on ferns and grasses, and on the ubiquitous planetary bananas. There were even Goro-nut desserts, wines and the famous whiskey, but no mention of *sqot* on any of the menus.

Jacoob had slipped away immediately the doors of the shuttle were opened, without a further word. It was better that whoever would be meeting Burk and Milliya didn't see the little Scribe. There were no formal disem-barkation procedures; that had all been taken care of on the control vessel. Each passenger was invited to go though a health scanner, though—these were too heavy and bulky to be installed in an orbiting space vessel—, and given a recorded briefing on the health dangers of Lemnos. The composition of the atmo-sphere, it was claimed, was slightly different to that of Terra, and it was therefore advisable to attend a health clinic in Lemnos City once a week to receive medication to counteract the negative effects of breathing in too much (or too little) of this or that.

Burk remarked that this would make it difficult for them to go undercover on Lemnos.

Milliya said: "Rubbish. If we register at a health clinic we'll both be arrested within a week." And there was no good reason to register. The atmosphere of Lemnos was much healthier than the polluted muck that passed for air on Terra. And, as she explained, the "medication" was a placebo. The whole procedure was intended to make visitors to Lemnos feel that they were being looked after by a benevolent Government, and also to give the Government a sneaky way to keep an eye on visitors. None of the settlers bothered with the medication and, after trying unsuccessfully to force them to, the Government had adopted the official line that the settlers' bodies had miraculously "adjusted" to the slightly different atmosphere of Lemnos.

Signs pointed the way to different exits, including the transport stations for public shuttles and the parking lot for private ones. First, though, all the arrivals had to have a final identity scan, passing through a narrow electronic gate where a pair of particularly nasty-looking Guardians, doubtless more efficient than Guardian Georgeena, had one last chance to peer at them and confirm that they were indeed the individuals the passenger lists said they were.

Beyond the gate, a noisy mob of loved ones, hosts, and drivers peered at the arriving passengers. Someone in that crowd was looking, quietly and intently, not for the "Guardian Jo-anna" and "Markko Mann" detailed on the passenger lists, but for Burk and Milliya.

CHAPTER THREE
MEETINGS...

"SO THIS IS THE MAN named 'Mann', who claims to be a media technician—am I right, Mr. Burk?"

He was slightly smaller than Burk, and maybe twice his age, but in peak physical condition, with broad shoulders and strong legs, and with hefty biceps bulging under his jerkin. The hand that he extended was huge and rough-skinned. His hair was cropped to a practical stubble, and his face was weather-beaten. He grinned, his eyes twinkled, and Burk thought: what does "thuggish" look like, then? Or "degenerate"? He could probably like this man, if he didn't already know what, and whom, he represented. He was a settler; a rich farmer.

"Yes, John Burk. John."

"We share the same first name, John, though *my* parents chose it spell it in a more orthodox way, J-O-N-N. We'll call you 'Burk' if we may? To avoid confusion. And this, I assume, is your charming Guardian accomplice—"

"Milliya."

No hand was offered this time. It would be forward,

even insulting, for a UsePop, however wealthy, to offer his hand to a Guardian, however junior. The other way around would also be unusual.

"Guardian Grade I Milliya Jahangiri. Only Grade I, but very promising, they say! You see how well-informed we are. Guardian Rebek'a has told me a lot about you. She herself will be returning on the *Starstretcher*, and so unfortunately will not be joining us. Perhaps you have a message from her?"

"No, only that the plan continues as agreed. She asks you to extend your full cooperation to Burk and myself, especially to Burk, because he will later be delivering a report, or giving evidence, in a certain matter."

The farmer laughed. He had beautifully made artificial teeth, like those of a pleasure android, which must have cost him a fortune. He was such an impressive physical specimen that, for a second or two, Burk played with the idea that he might even *be* an android—but androids didn't age, and they didn't build them to look sixty years old. Programming them to speak freely and conversationally was also very difficult.

"Whatever is needed! Burk and I are going to be such good friends. Ask for whatever you want. *My* home will be *your* home. And of course it won't all be work!"

He glanced at the small cases that Burk and Milliya were carrying.

"That is all your luggage?" ("Yes.") "Good. Sensible travelers. My personal shuttle is waiting for us, and our cooks are preparing supper. The estate is famous for its hospitality. You must be hungry! In any case, we shouldn't spend too long standing about in public. Both of you are here with false identities, and Burk is an escaped detainee, is he not? The friendly Guardians at the office of the Planetary Governorate would be very interested to meet him."

Burk smiled. "I expect they would."

"And as chance would have it, the office of the Planetary Governorate is precisely where I am off to now—to rescue my wife! She was on the *Starstretcher* with you, but with *rather more cases*. So many, in fact, that there was a little matter of excess baggage, a considerable amount of it, to be paid for. The spoils from her shopping expeditions on Terra and Luna! When the nice Guardians requested payment, however, she became somewhat emotional, and I've been told that at least one Guardian is now undergoing medical treatment."

"We don't like people hitting us, you know."

"I *do* know that, Guardian Milliya." He shrugged. "This is going to be very expensive for me—and not just because of the excess baggage. You don't mind if I ask you to wait here for a few moments while I deal with it?"

As the farmer strode off on his rescue mission, Burk caught himself thinking that there was something not quite right about the man. His slightly facetious manner didn't fit his rough-hewn appearance. One of the two was surely fake, was being put on for their benefit? Then he remembered how, back in the early days of the movie industry before androids took over, many of the most virile-seeming leading men were complete pansies in real life. Perhaps Jonn was also like this?

Whatever transaction took place between the farmer and the irate Guardians, it was done speedily, because very soon a convoy of robot baggage buggies, each transporting several garishly colored cases, was wending its way towards Burk and Milliya from the other end of the main hall. Behind the buggies followed a procession of humans: the owner of the luggage, once again proud mistress of her purchases; her husband, Jonn, looking rather less pleased; and a clutch of half-a-dozen dark-skinned, excited children, each holding a small bag. Burk's heart sank when he realized who the aggressive shopper and Guardian assailant was— Gloriya!

Gloriya was the retired movie starlet whom Burk had been sent to interview on board the *Starstretcher*. Inflamed by the consumption of two-thirds of a bottle of Goro-whiskey, the voluptuous but bulky former glamor queen had thrown herself at her interviewer, and Burk had fled for his life. The children were presumably the fruits of her other hobby (apart from shopping): charity work. Orphans from the slums of Manila or Greater Dhaka, they were on their way to adoption by bored, childless couples on Lemnos. The bags, containing all that they owned (or had been allowed to take with them), were in sharp contrast to the enormous baggage train of their benefactress.

Gloriya knew Burk's true identity, but then so did her

husband. She didn't know anything about the "Markko Mann" subterfuge, nor did she need to. Depending on how much she remembered about their romantic encounter, she could be a cause of embarrassment to Burk, but not of danger—not until the "WANTED" announcements began to appear on the news and recreational media. Then her loyalty to her husband would become important, and she might have to be told more.

In the event, she made no pretence at all of not knowing Burk, but clasped him to her ample bosom. This time there was no escape for him.

"Darling, this is the lovely man who wrote that wonderful article about me for *Onboard Personalities*! All about my selfless work for charity. We're going to take him home with us, aren't we, and have lots of fun with him!"

Then she spotted Milliya: "Why does he need a Guardian? Has he been arrested, like me? Traumatized? Brutalized? Darling, I swear, if they had been men I'm sure they would have raped and sodomized me. Probably with their tasers...."

"No, my dear, I tried to explain it to you a moment ago...." (and he went on to explain once again who their two guests were and that they would be staying for a while and exploring the countryside around the estate).

"Well, it will be fun to have a new girl around the house," she finally said to Milliya, "our regular guests are so *boring*, and you don't have to wear that frightful uniform, do you? I'm sure you have some lovely outfits with you!"

Milliya pointed immediately to her tiny case.

"Then I shall dress you in some of mine." Anticipating the remark that her husband was about to make, she added: "You don't need to say anything nasty about the size, darling! I still have a lot of the stuff from my movie days. They would fit—what was your name again?—of course, Milliya! But my new purchases would naturally be a teeny-weeny bit too large."

With her husband grimacing behind her back, she made an expansive gesture towards her new purchases, which took in not only the buggies but also the group of orphan children.

"Oh, yes, *them*. Poor, disadvantaged creatures, plucked by my organization from hell-holes in the poorest parts of Terra and now destined for happy, loving homes. Don't worry, they won't be coming with us in the shuttle, gabbling all the way and dirtying the seats. I've arranged for them to go on a public shuttle later on. They won't get lost: they have nowhere else to go to, and they know how much we love them, poor darlings."

The settlers' private shuttle was large and comfortable. The estate, too, when they arrived, spoke of affluence. Its main buildings, stores and outhouses sprawled across a massive chunk of the gloomy Lemnian plain. Although it was presumably a farm, apart from a few fields of ferns and a clump of Lemnian bananas there was barely any vegetation. Burk was now fully convinced that his hosts were extremely wealthy people, but how could the estate survive, even flourish, without crops? How did they make a living (let alone turn a profit)?

They had passed by several other, though smaller, estates, each surrounded by a similar but larger patch of green. In-between: mile upon mile of gray-brown aridity. Jonn had made a point of telling Burk how the Government had ordered the vegetation to be stripped, and forced the settlers to do most of the dirty work themselves.

"It was *sqot*. Well, not entirely—there were islands of other plants. *Sqot* likes a bit of variety. It doesn't like to be on its own."

He had grinned at the thought. Burk was finding it difficult to reconcile what Gloriya had told him (complainingly and at length) about her "elderly business husband" with the figure of the tanned, muscular farmer sitting beside him in the shuttle. As a movie starlet, she would have done well enough for herself; and as a comfortably well-off UsePop Breeder she could have had her pick of male Consorts. She had chosen an older man, but a fit, good-looking one. And it must be *his* wealth that was paying for the estate, and for the shopping sprees, and for the generous charity activities—she can't have made *that* much money in her movie career. So why had she run him down so scornfully to the young information officer sent to profile her for the *Starstretcher*'s onboard magazine?

It would soon be time for cocktails. Holding a reception for new arrivals was apparently one of the rituals of the estate. Burk and Milliya would apparently be the stars of the show, the center of attention. The little orphans had not been invited, although Burk knew that they had arrived. He had heard the surface shuttle that brought them, and the sounds of their voices and of other, more adult voices, as their pathetic belongings were unloaded. He couldn't see them from the window of his guest-room, but it was a peculiarity of Lemnos that sounds carried enormous distances. They could have been a long way away, on the other side of the estate.

Burk and Milliya had been given separate guest-rooms on the first floor of one of the main buildings, just a couple of doors apart. They couldn't share a room. She was a Guardian; he was only AdPop. The strata were not supposed to mix. If she wanted to take physical advantage of him that was fair enough— these things happened, didn't they, the universe wasn't perfect—though such behavior tended to be frowned upon, and it wouldn't help her professional advancement. Any suggestion, though, that *he* was preying on *her* would be tantamount to a death sentence. (Not formally, of course, but one night an off-duty, out-of-uniform death squad of Guardians would pay him a visit....)

In contrast, the outward signs of their being in a stable relationship—such as their sharing a room, for example—would have provoked among Milliya's Guardian colleagues pity rather than outrage but would also have had consequences. Burk would be transferred to some distant mining outpost. She would likely be invited to give up her Guardian status and move into a different area of work, some kind of job more in keeping with her apparent emotional unreliability: assistant in a kindergarten, say, or deputy manager of a canteen.

"Where you choose to *sleep* is up to you," Jonn had said, once again with his trademark grin. "We're easy-going folk, as you may have noticed. And the members of our staff are discreet. But guests come and go, and visitors look in to make deliveries. It's best to be careful. Cocktails in the reception room, in one hour's time? An opportunity to meet the other guests."

He stopped in the doorway, and turned.

"Oh, and there's one guest that I think you already know, someone else who was on the *Starstretcher*. Someone that I didn't want to be seen with at the space-port. A little surprise for you. So don't be late, please. "

CHAPTER FOUR
...AND MATINGS

BURK AND MILLIYA went down to the reception room on time, but separately, so as not to appear to be a couple. On the way, Burk took several wrong turnings—deliberately. The estate was essentially a giant ranch, with the various buildings interlocking, sometimes at ground level, sometimes on a higher floor. There was also a complex of rooms on an underground level, or levels, he noted with interest, though he didn't dare to investigate them. If he was caught, he couldn't say that he was looking for the reception room: it would unlikely be located underground. This was still his best opportunity to snoop around a bit without arousing suspicion. Later he would be expected to know his way around, and it would be harder to explain why he happened to be somewhere where strangers weren't welcome.

Many of the rooms were functional-looking cubes rather than areas intended for living in. There were crates and containers in some of them, closed tight and with mechanical seals or even digital locks. They could contain farm produce, after all, this was supposed to be a farm, but why then such elaborate security? And there were none of the usual twigs, leaves, husks, stalks or other agricultural debris to be seen on floors or in corners. If the containers were full of farm produce, the contents had been packed elsewhere.

The sectors for living and entertaining were unmistakable. Everywhere you looked there were designs and artworks connected with or inspired by Gloriya's movie exploits. These were often in lurid colors and included twinkling, shining, glowing or stroboscopic effects. As a highlight, in the four corners of the spacious reception room there were larger than life holograms of Gloriya in what were presumably her most famous roles. (Burk didn't consider himself an expert.)

All the figures were voluptuous, with hologrammic exposure of heaving breasts and plump thighs. One character that Burk recognized was Nurse Meggan from *Kill for Love*, a movie that he had once been forced to watch. His then girlfriend had downloaded it onto his entertainment center without telling him, and then demanded that they watch it together—her idea of a cosy romantic evening—complete with all the expensive sensory add-ins.

Nurse Meggan was not the female lead. It was not *her* destiny to save the handsome, if infantile, junior doctor from the wicked Dr. Fell, a crazed Ciaranite SurPop who had inveigled his way onto the surgical team in order to murder and mutilate injured Guardians. The task of rescuing the doctor was reserved for the heroine of the movie, Guardian Dr. Goode, who thwarted and terminally tasered the filthy villain before riding off into the sunset (in her private shuttle) with young Dr. Who-ever (Burk was convinced that the undemanding male lead had been given to an android). Nurse Meggan's role involved her being repeatedly ravished by the bestial Dr. Fell and then hacked to death with sundry surgical instruments, each more evil-looking than the last.

Lulled to sleep in his girlfriend's arms by the inane plot and banal dialog, Burk was rudely awakened when she belatedly remembered to swich on the sensory effects: horrible smells, mild pain stimuli, and then the first of Nurse Meggan's many orgasms. Orgasm technology in the movies had evolved out of early twenty-first century cybersex engineering. It was unfortunately still the least satisfactory of the different sensory tricks that the movies offered. To be explicit, the electronically stimulated thrills in the genital department, if you were correctly hooked up, were (to Burk's mind) more than offset by the accompanying vibrations and shaking, leading to mild nausea—sensations similar to those that you would experience in a bad shuttle collision. He had switched off the sensories, to his girlfriend's great displeasure. Soon afterwards, she was his *ex*-girlfriend.

Too late! Burk had gawped in horrified fascination at the oversize Nurse Meggan for slightly too long. Although there were fifty or sixty people in the room, Gloriya had spotted him, and she pounced.

"I'm glad you like it. It was one of my finest roles. I gave it my *all*."

Burk nodded. The hologram's mighty breasts, the nipples thrusting through the flimsy material of the nurse's uniform (which was soon to be torn from her body), heaved and shuddered. Burk's stomach was churning (or was it from hunger?).

"Perhaps a drink?"

She clicked her fingers and an androgynous young waiter, almost prettier than the android that had played Dr. Who-ever in *Kill for Love*, appeared with a tray of drinks. Burk noticed that, barring a skimpy loincloth, he was naked. His body was painted and oiled.

"You'll try our banana special? If you don't like it, one of the other boys will still have some straight banana juice. Or some Goro-nut whiskey, if you aren't familiar with that yet?"

She clicked her fingers a second time, and another young man appeared with an even more heavily-laden tray of drinks. He too was very scantily dressed.

"You like our boys? These two are Colombians. They're pretty, aren't they? They were in the first batch that I brought back from Terra years ago. I couldn't bear to part with them, so they've stayed with me ever since! They do love me so. It was my idea to dress them exotically. It gives an extra touch to the atmosphere of the party."

"It certainly does."

She tilted her head to one side, and gave him an intensive look.

"Come on, Mr. Burk, you can't fool me: I know that you're not tempted by these particular fruits."

Then her eyes seemed to mist over—perhaps a trick that actresses learn, he thought. "Think back. I can remember it only too well—the touch of your hands on my breasts, when you came to interview me. Is that your normal interview style, Mr. Burk?"

Burk wasn't sure how to respond to that. He didn't want to be rude, but neither did he wish to encourage her—his escape the first time had been a close-run affair. And it hadn't been his hands on her breasts; more the other way round: her breasts on his hands. She now stepped closer into his personal space, seeking eye-contact (or worse). Then—thank goodness!—one of the house staff, more conservatively dressed, a steward maybe, distracted her with a question or a message, perhaps about the catering arrangements.

Burk looked around desperately. Milliya was over on the far side of the room, deep in conversation with Gloriya's husband. From a distance, it seemed to be a far more sedate encounter than the ordeal that Burk was going through. The settler was holding back politely, not interrupting her, and his posture was discreet and respectful. There was no indication that he was coming on to Milliya, making a play for her! He wouldn't dare, though: despite his wealth, she was a Guardian and he wasn't.

The other guests were a rainbow collection of the bronzed and the beautiful. "Sin City" seemed to have been stripped of its glittering people for the evening, as if they had all been shuttled out to Jonn's estate for the reception to make a bold statement about conspicuous consumption. Never (and definitely not on Terra) had Burk seen so many glowing tans and so much clunky jewelry (on the men, too), so much *risqué* cleavage, so many gold medallions on hairy chests. (Milliya, who knew about such things, told him afterwards that it might have been a "glamrock retro party". Burk didn't have a clue what she was talking about.)

It would be wiser not to seen with Milliya too much, even if (as Jonn had said) they were more or less "among friends". Nor to use their names too often, neither their real ones nor "Markko Mann" and "Guardian Jo-anna". His escape, and Milliya's defection, would already be known; descriptions and images might already be circulating in the Lemnian media; attractive bounties for information leading to their capture (or worse) might already be on offer. These guests, however, didn't look as though they needed the money, and nothing about them suggested "Government employee", let alone "Guardian". The greatest danger was Guardian Sousanna, whose stern beauty had immediately reminded Burk of the Greek goddess of wisdom. She was no doubt in Lemnos City somewhere—but this wasn't Pallas Athene's kind of party, and these weren't her sort of people!

The music had been playing at a low volume to enable conversation. Now the volume was increased, and the music became recognizable as vulgar late twentieth-century dance music. A few of the guests took to the dance-floor. Initially they danced in pairs, facing each other though without their eyes meeting, and hopping or sliding clumsily from one foot to the other. Some of the women danced together, but peered about them as they did so, their gaze turning like the beam of an old-fashioned lighthouse, either to see who was watching them or because they were looking for a potential partner of the opposite sex.

With a powerful shove in his back, Gloriya propelled Burk onto the dance-floor.

"You have been ignoring me for several minutes. That makes you a bad bad boy! Abracadabra, let's see what you can do...."

And off she went, moving every part of her body that could move and some other parts besides. Burk was quite unable to keep pace with her. He couldn't help noticing that Gloriya was putting her outfit under unbelievable pressure. He remembered the wardrobe malfunction on the *Starstretcher*, when one of her surgically enhanced mammaries had burst from its moorings. Here the danger was not only to the hydraulics of the upper level; down below, Gloriya's massive, curvaceous rear was straining against the constricting fabric of her dress. It had several splits in it, but these were apparently intended to reveal the wearer's physical charms rather than to make it easier for her to dance.

The first number segued into the second, and Gloriya's movements became even more dramatic. Burk looked across the room and found Milliya, now also dancing, her partner a midget gentleman with bouffant hair, a gold lamé shirt and platform shoes. He was moving surprisingly gracefully, though keeping her at a careful distance. Although Milliya was out of uniform—in fact, Gloriya had kept her promise and found an old outfit of hers from her movie days that was only *slightly* too large and not offensively brash—the settler's cronies had presumably all been informed that she was a Guardian, albeit a renegade one. Guardians were taught how to kill with their bare hands in First Year training. Female Guardians were known to be more adept in close combat, and—to compensate for their lighter body weight—more vicious than the males. Even an off-duty female Guardian might lash out violently at any hint of UsePop disrespect. If they could crack Goro-nuts between their fingers....

Gloriya was now bumping her torso up against Burk whenever the rhythm of the music allowed it, touching as much of his body with hers as she could. Her intentions in his direction were plain for anyone to see. Burk was beginning to worry about how to handle this situation. Was he prepared to go the whole way with Gloriya, to do the deed of darkness with her, if it was in the line of duty and the situation called for it? He wasn't so sure. He had escaped on the *Starstretcher*; would she let him out of her clutches a second time? And what would Jonn do if he caught them together *in flagrante*? Indeed, was he watching them now, and seeing his wife imitating the motions of sexual congress with Burk on the dance-floor?

The answer to that last question was quick in coming. Burk had lost sight of Jonn during the dancing, but suddenly he was there beside them, accompanied by a woman who was built like...a *building* rather than a human being, with immense shoulders, long arms and a face that was criss-crossed with scars. The ugliest woman that Burk had seen bar none, and bigger even than Guardian Rebek'a had been.

He said something to Gloriya—Burk couldn't hear what it was—and she slipped away.

"This is Leyna, my estate manager. She's SurPop, but I have absolute faith in her. Be nice to her, and she'll be nice to you! Tomorrow morning she'll take you and your lady friend to see what you've come to see. Can you hear me or do we need to go outside?"

"I can hear you."

"Your lady friend has already been told. You'll be leaving after breakfast. The days and nights are short here on Lemnos. So lay off the Goro-nut whiskey, and don't make *too* much of a night of it, whatever goodies may be on offer. Okay?"

"Okay."

Then he was gone.

Almost immediately, Gloriya was dancing with him again, though without her previous enthusiasm, as though she was aware of what her husband had said to Burk. After a few more dances, the music was interrupted for an announcement that the buffet supper was ready, in the adjoining hall. Gloriya led Burk through, but then left him to his own devices while she spoke to some of the staff who were serving the food.

The food was *not* reconstituted crap courtesy of the

Delicio Corporation. Nor was it the tasteless mix of rations and stale "real" food that most inhabitants of Terra consumed day in, day out. Everything was fresh. Everything that Burk tried was delicious. So this is how the rich live, he thought!

There were even meat dishes. Burk had read that there were some estates south of Lemnos City where, at great expense, livestock were bred. Some of the meat was baked with a honey glaze. Real honey! So there were bees on Lemnos, too. But where did they find their nectar? Surely it didn't come from *sqot*?

He had expected Lemnian standards like the ferns and mosses, but not that, properly cooked, they too could be so tasty. And the desserts were exquisite: banana-based blancmanges, jellies crusted with sugar, tartlets with a filling of Goro-nut paste. Jonn's boast about the reputation of the estate's hospitality had not been unjustified.

The guests were served with slavish dedication by the estate staff, attractive young men and women, many of them almost nude, who circulated among them, topping up their drinks and bringing them further titbits from the buffet table. Every need was clearly being attended to....

That was one impression that, later that night, Burk and Milliya found they could agree upon, as they exchanged impressions of what they had experienced during the evening. They were bedded down in Milliya's room, which they had returned to by separate routes so as not to arouse suspicion.

The staff ("slaves, more like it", was Milliya's comment) had provided every imaginable service to the guests. They had been the cooks and waiters, they had laid on a little concert of singing, juggling and acrobatics after the buffet, and they were even now clearing up and cleaning.

"But not all of them," said Milliya. On her way back to the guest-room she had seen several of the waitresses in intimate embrace with male guests. In the guest-rooms on the floor below a party that might better be described as an orgy was in progress. Open doors provided fleeting glimpses of a range of different ways of achieving pleasure, in pairs or in a group. In one room, a naked girl was being mounted by Milliya's bouffant-haired dancing partner while another man waited to take his turn with her.

"Unmistakable," she said, "No-one else has hair like that. You know, he was an excellent dancer—so I'm surprised that he still had the energy!"

There were some same-sex couplings, too.

"But I didn't see Gloriya. She's saving herself for you, darling! Or her husband has got her on a leash tonight."

Burk was being unusually quiet. She prodded him.

"Don't you think? Or would you rather be in bed with her than with me?"

Burk looked at her with unexpected seriousness.

"No. He hasn't got her on a leash. And I understand now why he doesn't really care what his wife gets up to. You see, on my way up here *I* noticed a few things too. I saw our host taking his pleasure with someone who most definitely isn't his wife."

"One of the waitresses?"

"No. That wouldn't worry me. It was someone from the *Starstretcher*. He had warned me. There was no mistaking the fact that they have a close and intimate relationship. It was no casual screw. Perhaps they've been working together for longer. Perhaps they're a couple."

"Yes, so: who was it?"

"It was the lovely Dhavid. You remember him? The crewman that Guardian Adriyan was bedding—until Guardian Adriyan got murdered by your girlfriend."

CHAPTER FIVE
A DAY IN THE COUNTRY

HOURS LATER they were still mulling over Burk's chance discovery. They had had sex, of a sort, though it was not very satisfactory for either of them, as they were both distracted by the thoughts racing through their heads. The possibility that Dhavid might be working for Rebek'a and her settler friends gave them no peace. They had managed only a few hours' sleep.

"What's really strange is that Dhavid complained to me—you know, he was my neighbor when we went into the transportation pods—about how Guardian Adriyan was much too old for him, how he was cramping his style socially, costing him his reputation. And then a few days later he steps out with a man twice his own age."

"'Stepping out' isn't *quite* how I'd describe what you said you saw them doing! I didn't know that men did it like that.... Ugh!"

Burk didn't want to pursue that particular line of discussion.

"Did Dhavid betray his lover? Rebek'a knew that Guardian Adriyan would be visiting me in the holding cell, telling me things that I shouldn't be told. So, who told *her* that he would be there?"

"Scribe Jacoob also knew—"

"We can trust him. At least, I hope we can."

"Maybe. Who knows. But look: Jonn *warned* you that there would be someone from the *Starstretcher* among the guests. He wouldn't have done that if they already suspected us. Maybe they're working together, maybe they just happen to be lovers—but who cares? What matters is that they still think *we're* working for them. Remember: Rebek'a's original plan was that we should do exactly what we're doing right now: letting the settlers brief us on all the dirty stuff that the Government have been getting away with on Lemnos. She only changed the plan, spontaneously, to have *me* working on the planet and *you* travelling back to Terra with her, when she realized that I didn't trust her. It was an improvisation, she said so herself. Now she's dead, and no-one knows about it except us!"

He nodded.

"Alright, you're saying we can relax. What we *have* learnt is that our settler friend is cleverer and better-informed than we thought. And that our handsome crewman is probably a treacherous rat. I don't feel much like relaxing."

But they still did, sleeping for another hour before dressing and going down to the breakfast room.

Leyna was waiting for them, sitting in front of a great mound of breakfast remains: crusts and crumbs, fruit-skins, leftover cereal. She was a big girl: she needed her breakfast! After the huge buffet the evening before, Burk wasn't particularly hungry, but he couldn't help noticing that there wasn't a tablet or concentrate packet in sight—it was fresh produce only.

"Does all this come from the farm?" he asked Leyna.

"Some."

"But we didn't see much land under cultivation. Is the food harvested much further away?"

"Maybe."

"It's a big estate," ventured Milliya.

"Yes."

"How big?"

She shrugged.

Leyna was not a talkative person, as they continued to notice throughout the day. She told them what needed to be said, without extra commentary, and otherwise her answers to their questions tended to be monosyllabic.

She showed them—without speaking—how to strap themselves in to the shuttle, which was not the usual people transporter, but a large, dirty, multi-functional vehicle with only a few seats and a lot of space for freight. Once again, though, there were no indications in the form of agricultural litter that the shuttle had recently been used for transporting anything agricultural.

They drove out across the Northern Lemnian Plain through a landscape that was almost totally barren. The patches of cultivated ground were few and far between, and they didn't see anyone at all working the crops. The shuttle hovered, suspended on jet-drives, so no roads or tracks were needed. It followed invisible transit lines, unmarked except for tiny direction receivers embedded in the surface at regular intervals. Even these were probably unnecessary, as there was an onboard navigation system. Occasionally they saw the buildings of other farms or estates in the distance, but Leyna gave no sign that they would be visiting anyone during their trip.

The shuttle was impressively fast. After a few hours they had traveled an enormous distance, but still without any noticeable change of scenery.

Milliya had been calculating the distances and the direction.

"Are we going to the Other Side? You know, 'Limbo-Limbo-Land'"?

Burk thought: Limbo-Limbo-Land could hardly be much emptier than the country they had been traveling through for several hours. His bottom was beginning to get sore.

"No."

"But we *are* going in that direction?"

"Yes."

"How close to the Other Side will we be going?"

Then the dam broke. "Don't ask questions! I have to concentrate. This is *difficult*."

Actually, it wasn't. Milliya had been trained to drive shuttles, and she had been watching Leyna. Compared with some of the military hardware the Guardian had learnt to drive, this one looked quite easy. It even had an old-fashioned mechanical ignition key, rather than modern keyboard ignition. It was *so* much easier to tweak a mechanical setup than it was to override ignition software! (Although Milliya could probably do that too if required.) She stored away all these impressions for possible future use. You never knew, it might even be necessary for her to drive this beast one day.

Leyna had said that it was "difficult". Since driving the shuttle *wasn't*, what did she mean? Had she been given a difficult or unpleasant job to do: like driving them out into the wilderness and then murdering them? Surely their cover hadn't already been blown? Though killing them would hardly be necessary, it would be enough just to dump them in a particularly arid stretch of countryside and leave them to die of thirst. More likely her instructions were to take them to look at some bit of fakery—a heap of dead *sqot*?—and tell them: "The Government is responsible for that."

No, that sentence was too long for Leyna, she'd just say: "The Government."

Milliya's musings were interrupted by a slurping sound. Burk was gulping down a Lemnian banana, looted from the breakfast buffet.

"Would you like one?"

"No thank you."

She was quite annoyed. While *her* mind had been hard at work—this could turn into a life-or-death situation for them—*his* had been focused on food, with the rest of his brain switched off! Typical AdPop.

"Are you hungry?"

That was three words....

"We'll stop. Lunch."

At the back of the shuttle was a proper lunch hamper, which Burk and Milliya had completely overlooked. Milliya was angry with herself. They mustn't fall into the trap of seeing only the obvious, of noticing only things that they were looking for or were invited to notice. When the time came they might *have* to be able to see, perhaps in only a fraction of a second, some important secret that the enemy desperately wanted to be kept hidden.

The hamper was full of goodies. They particularly appreciated the banana-flavored water and the juices, kept cool in chill-containers. It was now quite warm, with the light, slightly red-tinged by Zora, shimmering as the air heated up. Out here on the plain, Milliya thought, thirst would definitely be the problem, not hunger.

Would they be able to handle Leyna, if it came to violence? *She* might be able to, despite the estate manager's massive size and strength; Guardian training prepared you to deal with any kind of opponent. But Burk would be worse than useless. The idiot had stood up to Rebek'a bravely enough—Rebek'a, rather smaller than Leyna, but infinitely more dangerous—and together they had somehow been able to overwhelm her. No, it was the *sqot*: *that* had made the difference, though how it had happened was still a mystery to her. And they wouldn't be so lucky a second time.

If it came to violence, she must make her move

before Burk was involved, because Leyna would break him in seconds. Break him so badly, perhaps, that no repair would be possible.

As their picnic lunch proceeded, Milliya found that her speculations about a showdown with Leyna were beginning to look more and more improbable. There was something about sharing good food with people that made the idea of having to fight or kill them soon afterwards seem almost ridiculous. They packed what was left of their lunch back in the hamper, not because the estate was short of food but simply out of habit.

"Now I give you something."

It was the longest sentence that Leyna had spoken all day. She led them back to the shuttle and pointed to a communication device fixed to the dashboard.

"Master said: copy this."

Master? Burk and Milliya exchanged glances. It was unheard of for a woman to use such a word to refer to a man.

"Switch it on. *Here.* Copy it."

She showed Milliya the controls for switching on the device—it was a planetary model that Milliya hadn't seen before—and then got out and walked away in the direction of a single stunted bush some distance from the shuttle. Did she want to have a midday snooze? Or go to the toilet? Or was she leaving them alone together so that they could follow her "Master"'s instructions?

Milliya brought out her own personal communicator, but before she could switch it on—

"Stop! This is what Jacoob said we *shouldn't* do."

"And how am I going to transfer the data *without* swiching it on?"

The two communicators could be plugged together, so there was no need for an ether transfer, but they did both have to be switched on.

"You heard what he said: if you switch it on, and the Government track it, within moments there'll be a big fat drone heading our way. Or a Guardian hit-squad. Don't take the risk, don't switch it on...*unless we hit gold*. And this is not gold. This is some faked-up stuff."

"Then let's take a look at it."

Milliya switched on the other communicator. There was no danger in that. It was unlikely that anyone would be trying to track a communicator in one of Jonn's estate shuttles. She peered at the display.

"There are images. Faked, we may assume. And some transcripts. Lots of text. Interviews, maybe, affadavits, sworn statements: what kind of stuff would be needed for a judicial enquiry? A huge judicial enquiry to bring down the Government?"

"It may all be worthless."

"Yes, but clever lawyers can sometimes make gold out of dross like this. I'm going to copy it."

Burk was indignant: "What? And help them in their rotten scheme?"

"Darling, switch your brain back on. She's watching us now, want to bet? What happens if we *don't* make a copy? 'Master' is not going to be pleased."

"It's too dangerous. Remember what Jacoob said."

"No, I don't think so. Why have they taken us on a

day trip into the depths of the pampa? For sightseeing? I don't see any sights. For fresh air? We could have made copies quite comfortably back at the estate."

Now Burk realized what she was saying.

"But *out here*, on the other hand—"

"—out here we're a long way from the tracking station at Lemnos City. Perhaps even beyond its range. Of course, they may have tracking satellites, but will they be set to monitor *this* quadrant? Teeming, as you can see, with life and subversive activity? A Ciaranite behind every bush? And have we seen more than ten bushes all day? No, we were brought here deliberately, and so I think we should do them the honor."

With a dramatically loud click—loud enough for Leyna to hear, if she was anywhere nearby—she clipped the two communicators together, switched on her own device, and began the copying process.

"You'll notice that I'm not checking 'Guardian Jo-anna''s messages and alerts. That really would be asking for trouble."

At exactly the moment that Milliya disconnected the communicators they were rejoined by Leyna.

"We leave now."

On the way back, she gave them an impressive display of her physical strength. It all started when one of the jet-drives began to stutter and splutter, making the ride very bumpy indeed. They came to a halt, and Leyna switched off the power. The vehicle sank gently to the ground.

"You help," she said to Burk, and they got out of the

craft.

She soon found the fault, and showed him what needed to be repaired—it was a valve that had to be screwed tight—then gave him a spanner with which to do it. But the valve was almost completely underneath the shuttle, so that there was no chance of getting a good purchase on it with the spanner. To Burk's (and Milliya's) amazement, Leyna gripped the side of the craft with one hand *and lifted it up.*

"Do it," she said.

Although he had to wriggle precariously under the shuttle, at no point did he get the feeling that she might be about to let the vehicle slip out of her hand and come crashing down on him. Not even when he fumbled and cursed and took longer than he should have done.

"Good," she said afterwards, with no show of emotion. "Good." And they drove on.

During the remainder of the return journey, Leyna barely spoke. She had carried out her instructions and was now delivering the two guests back to the estate. What further need was there for social pleasantries? The days were shorter on Lemnos than on Terra, but they arrived back well before dark.

They found Gloriya fussing about in the reception area of the central building.

"I hope you enjoyed your trip? And that you found what you wanted to see? My husband did say something, but I can't remember what it was. Some *more* new guests have come, as you'll notice at supper, but no-one important, so, please, no fuss! However, some nasty Guardian is coming tomorrow, from Lemnos City. (No offence, dear!) Jonn is not at all happy about that, as you can imagine, but he'll tell you himself. He's round the corner there in the estate office."

As they approached, they could see through the glass front that Leyna was already there, talking to her "Master"—or rather nodding, grunting and muttering in response to his questions. He turned to them as they entered.

"A good day? A useful trip, or so I've heard?" He didn't wait for an answer. "Fine. Let me know if there is more that you need."

Burk felt that it might be a good idea to make a show of interest.

"Perhaps an area that has recently been cleared of—"

The settler stiffened noticeably, and gave Burk his full attention.

"—of the *you-know-what*?"

"Ah, yes, let's avoid specifics, *please*, we don't know who might be listening, do we?"

"And a meeting with someone who was actively involved in the process?"

"Of course! No problem. Burk...*Guardian*...perhaps it's time to freshen up a little for supper? And for partying? I'm sure we'll find plenty of opportunity to explore these topics further. And I have some news that might interest you. But now, if you'll excuse me, Leyna and I...."

After they had been shooed out of the office, they took separate routes to the guest-rooms. This time they had agreed to meet at Burk's room. In keeping with his lower status, it was smaller than Milliya's, but since it had only a small window to an inner light shaft it would be harder to keep under surveillance, should anyone be suspicious of what its occupant was up to.

AdPops and trained Guardians have very different ways of entering rooms. If it had been Milliya who had gone in first, she would not have been taken by surprise so easily. She would for example have noticed that the lighting *didn't* go on automatically within one-and-a-half seconds of the door being opened.

Burk was pulled inside the room. A familiar voice whispered, "You too, my lady. Come in quickly and shut the door."

CHAPTER SIX
WELCOME AND
UNWELCOME VISITORS

"SWITCH ON THE LIGHTING. Quickly. It would look strange if it didn't go on now. I switched it off manually. But activate the blinds as well. After all, you've come back to the room for a quick one before supper, haven't you? And naturally you don't want any voyeurs."

Scribe Jacoob was still standing to one side of the small window, where he would only be visible from outside, at a very acute angle, by someone clinging to the outer wall.

"Good. We should be safe. It's *your* room that they'll likely be watching, my dear Guardian, not his. *If* they're watching. And the room is clean—I've scanned it for bugs."

He moved away from the wall and sat himself on the room's solitary chair. Burk and Milliya sat on the bed, holding hands. Yes, a quickie *had* been their intention, but there was no need to tell him that.

"We weren't expecting to see you quite so soon, Mr. Scribe, if at all—"

"*Jacoob*, please, Mr. Burk. It was the name I was

given, and my lowly professional function has no bearing on our...cooperation."

Milliya grinned and punched Burk playfully in the side. "He has no manners, the AdPop lout! What he meant is that we're *both* very happy to see you again, Jacoob. But a tiny bit surprised, perhaps?"

"Changes in circumstances may require changes in plans." He looked from one to the other. "How are they treating you here?"

"Everything's fine, Jacoob." Burk still found it very strange to use the little hunchback's name. "You said that they were degenerate and thuggish?"

Milliya laughed. "We had a glimpse of 'degenerate' last night, didn't we, darling?"

Burk laughed. The Scribe didn't.

"They can do 'thuggish' as well, believe you me." He paused to let the words sink in. "I thought you would be safe here. Now I think you *won't* be, and that's why I've come."

Burk gripped her hand more tightly.

"Has something happened?"

The Scribe tilted his head in acknowledgement rather than answering directly.

"Mr. Burk, have you managed to carry out the, er, *researches* that Guardian Rebek'a originally asked you to?"

"Yes, we have. They've given us material, and plenty of it."

"And do they have any further plans for you?"

"No, it seems not. We suggested going out to look

at an area that had been cleared of *sqot*, and talking to someone who was involved. But the settler—"

"Jonn. I know his name, Mr. Burk. Only too well."

"Jonn wasn't really interested."

"No, *sqot* was cleared around here a long time ago. Unless you were a soil expert with fancy measuring equipment you wouldn't be able to prove anything. Where they're probably still clearing it is on the Other Side. They won't want you to go *there*! Has anyone offered to take you?"

"No."

"Not particularly surprising. But that is where you'll have to go, sooner or later."

Burk didn't much like the sound of that, but didn't say anything.

"So, he had all the lies and faked evidence ready for you! He doesn't want you talking to anyone, though. They'll have what they claim are witnesses ready for the enquiry, but they'll need to prime them very carefully first. They're being cautious. They no doubt think that in your profession—I mean *John Burk*'s profession, not '*Markko Mann*''s—you would be able to spot a crooked witness, to see through their lies."

"Oh, I don't know...."

Milliya laughed. "Your modesty is fully justified, darling! But *they* don't know that. They're assuming that you're a big, big expert. They don't know you as well as I do!"

"Thank you for that."

"My pleasure."

"So, as far as *they* are concerned, you are finished here, Mr. Burk. Both of you, in fact. That's good. 'The Moor has done his job; the Moor can go.'"

"I beg your pardon?"

"Schiller, some old German writer. I'm surprised: I thought that you minored in Literature, Mr. Burk? I like books too. You know, my family originally came from Germany, before an event called the Holocaust." He paused. "What it means is this: that you could go quickly, tomorrow perhaps, without attracting too much suspicion. There would simply need to be an *explanation* for your sudden departure...."

"Jacoob, you haven't answered his question." She leant forward, looking at the Scribe intently. "What has happened? Why do we need to run?"

"What would you like first: the bad news, or the *very* bad news? The vague, or the specific? The imminent, or the distant threat? The merely frightening, or the terrifying?"

"How about the *imminent* threat?"

"Well chosen, Mr. Burk, because that is what is going to affect your immediate travel plans, and provide us, most conveniently, with the *explanation* that we need for your departure. Another guest will be arriving tomorrow, from Lemnos City."

"Yes, Gloriya said as much."

"This is someone that you met on the *Starstretcher*, but whom you won't want to meet here: Guardian Sousanna."

"Oh no!" Burk and Milliya groaned almost in unison.

The Scribe couldn't help laughing. "Don't be so unkind! Surely the universe is big enough to contain both you and her? She is an intelligent, hardworking servant of the Government, and a woman of integrity. What is wrong with that?"

"Can't she take her integrity somewhere else? Like, say—the Other Side?"

"I apologize for Burk. What he wants to know is: why is she here so soon? Is she on our trail?"

"No. Even though it's my privilege to tell you that you now have the status of Wanted Persons. Officially. But no-one among the settlers will give you up to the Government. Nevertheless, if Guardian Sousanna should happen to find you here, she will be obligated to arrest you. Or, at least, to try. However, you are not the reason why she is coming here."

"What *is* the reason?"

"She has a brief from the Government to find out who is destroying *sqot*. In other words, she is hunting the same people that you are. Her personal motives may be honest and decent—I say 'may'—but those of the Government, I fear, probably aren't. You can't work together." He paused. "And you can't work at all if you're in a Government cell."

"Does she know that Burk and I are here?"

"No, I don't think so."

"Then why is she coming here?"

"Because Government spies have told her that Jonn and his wife are the richest settlers on Lemnos. And that Jonn may be one of the ringleaders in a conspiracy to destroy *sqot*. Or to steal it, which the Government would hate even more."

"Then we'd better be gone before she arrives."

"Agreed. And now perhaps you should go down for supper before they come looking for you? Lowly Scribe and unsightly person that I am, I was not invited to the feast. They don't like me. I managed to find a tiresome, bureaucratic excuse for coming to the estate, but they didn't appreciate the tax documents that I delivered—who ever does?—and they told me to leave tomorrow. And I must eat in my room, of course, away from their treasured guests."

"Then I'll bring you something tasty from the buffet!" Milliya got up from the bed. "I need to go to my own room for a moment. Oh, and what was the 'bad news', then?"

"That *was* the 'bad news', my lady. I'm afraid the 'very bad news' is something altogether different."

"Yes?"

"The 'very bad news' is that Guardian Rebek'a is still alive, and that she's coming for you!"

Milliya sat down again. It would be hard to say which of them—Burk or Milliya—looked more distraught. The temperature in the room was suddenly ice-cold.

"You said—"

"Yes, I know what I said, my lady."

"—that the waste bins on the *Starstretcher*—"

"—would be emptied immediately after takeoff. At T-speed. Against standard Galactic Navigational Law. With the expertly forged signature of the Commander.

And they *were* emptied. Guardian Rebek'a should have been sent into her own personal orbit around Lemnos. Into well-deserved oblivion."

"What happened?"

"An officious junior officer was worried that something toxic might be unloaded. He checked the bins, and found some rather unusual waste...."

"So she wasn't killed after all?" Milliya now looked seriously alarmed.

"My lady, let me remind you that it was *you*—*both* of you—who refused to kill her when you still had the chance. And very noble of you it was, too. The waste bin murder was *my* little plan, against your wishes, and it went wrong. They found her. According to my shipboard informant, she was taken to the Commander, where she kicked up an unbelievable scene. She screamed, and shouted, and stamped her foot, and demanded that the *Starstretcher* be turned around to take her back to Lemnos." He laughed. "Have you any idea what that would have cost? Naturally, he said 'no' and, since she doesn't outrank him, that was that. Also, I think he was angry about the illegal order that he'd absent-mindedly signed while he was so busy during docking. An embarrassing oversight. I'm a superb forger, by the way!"

"So how did she get back to Lemnos?"

"I don't know if she's arrived yet. But she got lucky. The *Starstretcher* docked with a freighter going in the other direction. They had a sick man on board, with a dangerous infection. The *Starstretcher* has better quarantine facilities than a freighter does. And the infection would be easier to treat back on Terra. They transferred him across, and while they were doing it your Guardian friend used the opportunity to smuggle herself onto the freighter. And now she's on her way! But there is good news...."

Burk, whose head had in the meantime sunk towards his chest in gloom, looked up, as Jacoob counted the points off on his fingers.

"One: she left her Guardian documentation behind. She may have it implanted, but they don't have that sort of scanner on a freighter. Only at the Gate.

Two: the captain of the freighter may well arrest her as a stowaway.

Three: he certainly won't let her make any transmissions; there is a strict regulation that freighter crewmembers aren't allowed to send personal messages. Let alone stowaways.

Four: the Commander of the *Starstretcher* may inform Lemnos of her erratic behavior, and recommend that she be taken into custody and investigated.

Five: freighters like that are fairly slow.

Six...aren't five enough, do you really need more than that? Oh dear, I see that you do! Okay, six: you have a head start on her. You should use it."

CHAPTER SEVEN
HIGH SOCIETY

NEITHER BURK NOR MILLIYA wanted to go to supper. What they had just learnt had somewhat spoilt their appetite. And Jonn had promised them "a *proper* party", whatever that was, "now that we're all friends and the work has been done." Burk feared that it might involve partner-swapping—there had been a lot of that going on on the *Starstretcher*, and while he had no objection to it in theory, the thought of actually doing it with Gloriya made him feel queasy, and the thought of doing anything with Jonn even more so.

Milliya, for her part, revealed an unexpected prudish streak: she said that she'd kill anyone, male or female, who laid an intrusive finger on her, though first she'd *break* all their fingers, one by one.

Nor did Burk look forward to meeting Dhavid again. Perhaps he had betrayed Guardian Adriyan. Maybe he was in league with the settlers, whatever they were up to. Milliya reminded him: Dhavid had disembarked just as they had. He wouldn't know more than Jonn did, and if Jonn said that they were helping him, the crewman would believe that. Or at least he would until

Guardian Rebek'a appeared, casting her dark shadow over all of them, from which point onwards Dhavid would hardly be the biggest of their problems.

But Rebek'a was days, weeks even, behind them, and might have a few problems of her own when she got to Lemnos. She could rely on her network of settler friends. But she might not be able to rely on Government support. She might even be classified as a renegade, an escaped detainee, like Burk and Milliya.

And what did *they* have? They had the outlines of a plan, but not much more than that. The plan was essentially Jacoob's, so for better or for worse they were now committed to trusting him, even though they couldn't be sure what his exact agenda was.

The plan went like this: they would leave before Guardian Sousanna arrived; make sure to keep well ahead of Guardian Rebek'a (on no account did they want to bump into *her*); somehow they would travel across to the Other Side to see what was happening there with regard to *sqot*; and they would aim to get back to Lemnos City for any one of a series of specific dates when ships (*Starstretcher*'s sister ship, the *Starspringer*, for instance) were scheduled to be docked at the Gate, waiting to return to Terra.

The time windows at the Gate of Lemnos for disembarking and embarking were always very narrow, but *someone* would meet them, Jacoob had said, and that *someone* would *somehow* get them onto the ship. It didn't sound exceptionally promising. Moreover, until that moment arrived everything else would be entirely *their* responsibility. They would be on their own, without even a hand taser, and hunted soon by almost everyone on the planet. They would need to be creative. The "what" of their plan might be straightforward enough; the "how" would be horribly difficult.

At the entrance to the main reception hall—Burk thought of it as the "Nurse Meggan Room"—they tried to walk in separately, but were immediately intercepted by their hosts.

"There's no need for that! We all know who you are, and you're among *friends*. Relax! At least for tonight. *Please*. Tomorrow will be different, unfortunately: we'll have a senior Guardian joining us, someone who is reputedly not so interested in the better things of life, for instance those refinements and diversions that we cultivate here on the estate. In other words: the woman is a *pain*. And to make it worse, she apparently believes that I am a political agitator, a subversive—"

"My husband the Ciaranite!"

"Hardly, my dear. But Guardian Sousanna will put a dampener on the party atmosphere, I'm sure of that. And we don't want her stumbling over *you two*, do we? So you need to be gone before she arrives, and to stay away for a few days. With a plausible explanation." He turned to his wife. "Darling? But keep your voice down."

"Yes, and that is *my* little contribution! With Leyna as your driver, you will be going on what the Terrans used to call a 'safari'. The shuttle is stocked with provisions for up to five days, the finest items that our kitchen can offer. There is no actual wild life on Lemnos, as you know, *so you'll take it with you.*"

"I beg your pardon?" Burk was genuinely puzzled.

The settler explained: "My wife is playing Goddess of Love again.... Whoever you pick up tonight gets to go on the 'safari' with you. Just give me their names, and I'll tell them. I've seen the admiring glances that you've been getting! They won't say no when I tell them that they've won the evening's 'special prize'. We've done this before. Of course, the other guests don't need to know what's happening. We don't want any jealousy, do we? And if questions are asked, nobody will be in a position to say too much."

"*I'm* jealous of them already, darling! It will be such a lovely experience. You could say that you're taking the 'big game' (I believe that's the expression) with you in the shuttle!"

"Just one thing," her husband added, "Don't expect Leyna to join in."

Burk and Milliya *hadn't*. Gloriya burst into peals of laughter, as though she had just been vouchsafed a glimpse of the estate manager in vigorous action.

"*That* would certainly make the party go with a swing! A once in a lifetime experience? But even without her, it will be a wonderful trip. Think of it as an extension of this evening's entertainment. And just imagine it: camping out under the Kallipygian Moons, watching Zora rise and set, picnicking out on the plain, making love. How romantic! It could almost be the plot for one of my movies! I wish I could be going with you, but my absence would undoubtedly be noticed."

"Undoubtedly, darling. Whereas the absence of a couple of our guests wouldn't be. After all, our distinguished visitor hardly knows Lemnos, or Lemnian society, and she'll be on her own. If she happens to ask about Leyna: well, she's touring the estate. That's what an estate manager does, isn't it? Leyna will have her personal communicator with her—so we can call you back in at any time, once the coast is clear. But it shouldn't take us too long to get rid of our puritanical guest. She won't like it here one little bit!"

"If she outstays her welcome, I'll organize a themed party specially for her, based on one of my movies, perhaps, with nice costumes and role-plays. How about: 'Sex and violence'! That'll send her running!"

As far as Burk could remember, *all* of Gloriya's movies were about sex and violence, but he refrained from pointing it out.

"Don't worry, Burk, we'll drive her away long before you get back. But you should leave later tonight. Enjoy the party first, though, and don't forget to pick your partners for the 'safari'! One other thing—"

He handed them masks for the upper part of the face.

"Party rules for tonight. One of my wife's ideas. Not a full mask, because you'll want to eat—and to *kiss*. Besides, everyone can see who is behind the mask, can't they? It's just psychological; something to hide behind. Let all the inhibitions out! It's safer than using pills."

Gloriya whispered something in her husband's ear

that obviously amused him.

"Guardian, you look enchanting this evening, if you don't mind my saying so, but you're wearing the same outfit that you wore last night."

That was true—in both cases. Nor was Jonn the only person to have noticed how enchanting she looked. Little Mr. Bouffant Hair was standing close by, ogling her shamelessly. He had apparently lost his inhibitions of the night before, if the slight tenting at the front of his skin-tight outfit was anything to go by.

"Please go with my wife. She'll find you something more *appropriate* for tonight's party."

As the two women left, the settler turned to Burk: "So let the fun begin! The true predators, I suspect, have already picked out their prey. Have *you*?"

He ushered Burk into the reception hall, and then left him there to his own devices, predatory or other-wise.

There were more people at the party, Burk thought, than the night before. They would need two of them for the "safari". Not two for an orgy, though, as their hosts imagined, but two people who would be easy to handle, who could be intimidated, physically overcome, killed if necessary—though surely they wouldn't need to do that? Leyna, on the other hand, would be a very different proposition, and if it came to a fight with the estate manager, they couldn't afford to have anyone in the group who might give her active support.

Mr. Bouffant Hair was a possible candidate. He was encouragingly tiny and obviously vain and self-preoccupied, though that would have applied to most of the guests. With her Guardian training, Milliya would be able to subdue him immediately, and even Burk fancied his chances. Except for one thing. The man had *danced* so well: gracefully, and with such beautiful timing. He must be physically fit. Perhaps he did yoga? More to the point: perhaps he did martial arts?

Some of the other guests might be more suitable after all. Two *women*, perhaps? These were UsePop hedonists, not Guardians. Anyway, the choice would be Milliya's.

Now she returned, with Gloriya, who was clearly very pleased with what she had achieved, at her side. Burk's jaw dropped.

Milliya was wearing a diaphanous, pale lemon-colored top. Not much was left to the imagination. Her nipples pressed firmly into the thin material, even the areolae were clearly visible, and from the front you could see that her left breast was slightly larger than the right. They were of no more than average size, but were beautifully shaped. Whenever Milliya turned, their delightful roundness became even more apparent, almost inviting hands to cup and caress them.

As if that were not enough, Gloriya had put her into baggy pale blue pantaloons of a similar, almost transparent, fabric. The trousers hung loosely about her legs, while still hinting at the charming shape of her limbs. Around her hips, however, they were tight, exposing the curve of her buttocks and revealing that she was otherwise naked, except for a dark thong that at the back disappeared into the cleft of her bottom and at the front barely covered her mound.

None of this was unfamiliar to Burk, of course, but it would be a revelation to everyone else at the party. Milliya would certainly have no trouble finding someone who was eager to get to know her better. She would be able to take her pick! If anything, the problem would be: fighting them off.

She was wearing the small mask that Jonn had given her. The ironic juxtaposition that this created, of so much semi-naked loveliness, brazenly displayed, with the coy concealment of just the small area around her eyes, was hugely erotic. Burk noticed how Mr. Bouffant Hair was hovering towards her, moving in for the kill. So be it then, perhaps he's the one.

A few people were already dancing. The settler had taken to the dance-floor with Dhavid, and the two of them were circling each other, making elegant thrusting movements of their hips in time with the music. Occasionally Jonn reached out and stroked the handsome crewman's cheek or hair.

Burk thought: Why did Gloriya marry him? His leanings must have been obvious to her from the start. And she would have been familiar enough with men of his kind from the movie world, where those male stars that weren't androids tended to be gays. But the arrangement gave her freedom, too. Freedom to follow her own inclinations. And in an open marriage you do get to know more people!

Dhavid spotted Burk, and the two men stopped

dancing and came over to chat with him.

"We met on the *Starstretcher*," Dhavid told his partner. "You know, I could have had quite a thing for him. You see how cute he is. But he never even *looked* at me."

The settler's smile in response could have meant anything—or nothing.

"Dhavid thinks that life is a toyshop, but you can't always have the toys that you want, *when* you want them. Look over there, my dear. Burk has a pretty toy all of his own to play with, and she keeps him busy. Over there, Dhavid, *that's* his toy. Do you see what I mean?"

Dhavid looked across to where Milliya was dancing with her bouffant-haired admirer, and pouted.

"I have nicer legs than she does. And I can dance better than *either* of them." Dhavid's voice was getting very loud. "And do you know what? *I've* fucked a Guardian too!"

"Shut up, you little idiot!" Despite the fierceness, Jonn spoke in no more than a loud whisper. "Fucked a Guardian, or *been* fucked by one? There is quite a difference. Just keep your voice down. And be more respectful, or I'll ask her to come over and smack you."

Dhavid now looked suitably abashed.

"I'm sorry, Burk, I didn't think he would put you on the spot like this. These youngsters are so direct— they say what they think, and they say what they want. Still, at least you know now that you have an admirer. And if you do discover one day that your knife has a *double blade*, here's a good-looking young man who'd just *love* to be stabbed!"

Dhavid was indignant. "Daddy!"

"By the way, he goes off like a starship in hyper-drive. Though should you find that your taste runs to older men, well...."

"Daddykins!"

As he led his boyfriend back onto the dance-floor, the settler turned and winked at Burk, who thought to himself: Well, well, if that wasn't an interesting insight into the psychology of their relationship! *Daddykins!*

He scanned the guests on the dance-floor, but saw nobody who looked remotely suitable. The women were both over- and underdressed, their outfits combining a maximum of expensive vulgarity with the greatest possible flaunting of naked flesh. Not one of them was a patch on Milliya. Nevertheless, he would need to find one. She would have to be attractive enough to inspire him to flirt with her, to neck, fondle, stroke, grope—in fact, whatever it took!

He was confident that he knew well enough how to treat a lady. He *wasn't* confident that he knew how to fake being turned on, at least not so convincingly that his chosen lady would agree to go off on an extended sex party with him. He couldn't switch it on or off at will. He wasn't a horny teenager any more, and sex with Milliya had spoilt him.

There was another problem. Many of the women gave the impression that they wouldn't mind being pulled by a handsome young stranger—and Burk was

aware that there were women who found him attractive—but they weren't on their own. There were no
female singles in sight. Everyone seemed to have come
as half of a couple. And the men were all hefty, muscle-
bound settlers. The "drones" and "consorts" might not
be willing to surrender their partners to facilitate some
other man's fun and games; they could take the woman
and her partner together, but the men all looked as if
they might not be so easy to overwhelm; and, it did
need to be said, Milliya wouldn't fancy any of them!
Mr. Bouffant Hair was the man of her dreams in
comparison. Still, she'd have to do her duty, just like
Burk.

The easy solution would be for Jonn to delegate a
couple of his estate staff. He wouldn't agree to that,
though. If someone *did* start asking awkward questions, and he needed an alibi, if he needed to cover his
own tracks and deny his involvement, what could two
of his "slaves" possibly have been up to, escorting the
two wanted suspects on an elaborate sex "safari"?

Burk walked into the dining hall, where the buffet
had already been set up and the first guests where
circling the delicacies. It was much the same: couples;
men with muscles; women with elaborate outfits and
make-up.

He was on the brink of despair when the answer, the
key, the magic moment came. Was it a coincidence?
For some are born lucky, some make their own luck,
and some have their luck thrust upon them. (Burk was
sure that he had read that somewhere.)

Because there he stood, the solution to their problem, his charming lady wife Keesha beside him, both of them eyeing the food and munching on Lemnian banana canapés: Aylwin.

CHAPTER EIGHT
HOW *NOT* TO ORGANIZE
AN ORGY, PART ONE

AYLWIN WAS INITIALLY mildly alarmed to see Burk. Why was his ailing uncle not with him? Had the poor man's condition worsened? (The unspoken thought was: Let him not be anywhere nearby!) Burk was able to reassure him on that score. (He himself was thinking: Jacoob was not invited to supper, but let's hope that Aylwin doesn't bump into him on a staircase or glimpse him in a corridor.)

Aylwin's wife Keesha was small and friendly. Burk had been expecting a fearsome SM dragon, and was somewhat surprised. She was a distinct and rare physical type, what had once quaintly been known as "Afro-American". Generations of intermarrying between the so-called "races" meant that most people were now shades of pale copper, or olive, or dusky ivory, or light brown. Very dark or very white skin was extremely rare.

Rarest of all were Africans. Once there had been millions of them—far more than their impoverished continent could support—but that was before the

Troubled Times, with their regional wars, and the great Water Crisis, and the famines, and the Ciaranite Emergency. There was a rhyme that was chanted back then at demonstrations: "The poor are dead, The rich have fled, Give us justice!, Give us bread!" The demonstrators were given neither justice nor bread, only bullets and gas, and the Ciaranites were unable to prevent the mass triaging that followed, until there was scarcely anyone still alive in Africa between the Mediterranean and the Rainbow Country in the south.

Keesha could have passed for an African. Perhaps the descendent of rich refugees? Her name, however, was classic Afro-American. She and Burk laughed over the fact that they both had such traditional first names. They had hit it off quite well. Aylwin looked on admiringly as his wife made small-talk with Burk. After all his blustering at the Gate of Lemnos, Burk had not expected to find him in such an obviously happy and affectionate relationship. Even if it was an unorthodox one.

"My parents were *so* conservative! My mother was a top Guardian, and that's what was supposed to happen to me, too."

"It didn't work out, though?"

"No, I flunked school. My focus was on *forni*-cation, not *edu*-cation!"

She and her husband had an understanding, she said. They met each other's *needs*. Aylwin nodded enthusiastically. What these needs were was not further explained. In Aylwin's case, Burk thought that he knew, but Keesha?

She disappeared for a few minutes and Burk made his pitch. They had talked on the transfer shuttle about an "adventure holiday" on Lemnos, did he not remember? And through the generosity of their host, the dream was about to become reality. Jonn had said, "Take two good friends with you, have some fun, make it *romantic*." Could Aylwin and his wife imagine themselves...?

Aylwin beamed with pleasure. Yes, of course he could. He was greatly flattered, and would love to accompany his charming new friends on a little "safari trip", on which he might have the honor of getting to know a stern Guardian disciplinarian—intimately.

"And your wife...?"

She too would be delighted.

"Hmm. The arrangements could be...*complicated*. We don't want any unhappy misunderstandings."

That wouldn't happen! Keesha was absolutely *uncomplicated*—Aylwin pronounced the word very precisely—and she would be happy to assist Milliya in all activities, naturally she would, taking the opportunity to learn from a Guardian. He had already noticed, though, that she thoroughly enjoyed the company of Burk, and would undoubtedly like to see more of him.

Burk suspected a double entendre, though with Aylwin you could never be sure.

Keesha returned, and her husband whispered to her. While he was whispering, she didn't even for a moment take her eyes off Burk. When he finished, she stepped towards her new "friend" and looked up at him. Their eye contact was intense. When he and Milliya had sex, she always turned her eyes away from his when the moment came. This one wouldn't turn her eyes away.

"Yes, Mr. Burk, why not? It could be fun. Better talk to your girlfriend again, to make sure."

To bring Milliya over, Burk had first to detach her from her limpet-like admirer with the bouffant hair. He took this intrusion very amiss—had he imagined that this was the night when he would strike lucky?—and it was Milliya who quelled his indignation, not Burk, with whom Gylberto ("silly name, silly man" was Milliya's comment later that night) apparently wished to start a fight. ("And he would have won, darling, he's very fit.")

"So, you're trying to pimp me to our masochist friend from the Gate? Thank you, my dear, it's what I've always wanted!"

And when she saw Keesha, she said: "Not bad...I do declare. Mr. Burk, I rather think you're getting the better of this deal. How about I have some girlie fun with Mrs. Aylwin, and *you boys* do the bondage stuff? If you get bored, you can ask Leyna to help!"

Nevertheless, she was charm itself when the four of them discussed the trip, quietly, and standing apart from the other guests at the buffet ("We don't want to make anyone jealous, do we? This is our little secret"). There were no lewd jokes or dirty suggestions. Aylwin was plainly in awe of Milliya, now that he knew what the two of them might be doing together fairly soon.

Keesha was subdued, but kept her eyes on Burk.

Walking past, Jonn took in the little tableau at a glance. Arrangements were being finalized, it would seem. Burk and Milliya had made an interesting choice: Aylwin was known to have exotic tastes; his wife was reputed to be hot between the sheets. Several of Jonn's non-gay settler friends had tasted that particular fruit, and reported back very favorably.

The little circles of conversation broke up as more guests came into the hall, and people began to concentrate on the buffet. As on the previous evening, near-naked waiters with oiled and painted bodies circulated among the guests, carrying trays with drinks. This time there were also several bare-breasted waitresses. Milliya had asked Gloriya about the staff: not all of them were former orphans from her rescue project; some were SurPops, serving as indentured labor on Lemnos ("slaves", as Milliya had said).

Jonn spoke briefly to Aylwin and Keesha, but it wasn't necessary to talk to them for long—no-one had to be persuaded, and the arrangements were clear.

Burk and Milliya went to bed early, leaving the reception area separately soon after the entertainments had begun, with yawns and "It's been a long day" and similar comments. They met in Milliya's room to make their plans. There could be no errors—they had three people to deal with, one of whom was physically formidable, as they had already seen.

"Look in my bag, darling. I found them in one of the storerooms on my way back."

He opened the bag, and found coils of old-fashioned hempen rope.

"I made a little detour! It was risky, I know. I couldn't hide them. I can't hide *anything* in this costume, even my beauty spots! But we're going to need this stuff tomorrow, if we're going to play bondage games...."

"How do I...?"

"This is First Year Guardian training. I'll show you. And it's good that you don't know: it tells me that you don't do this as a hobby, my dear."

There was a tap at the door. Burk closed the bag. It was Aylwin. He looked rather disappointed to see Burk there as well as Milliya—had he been hoping to start the fun and games a bit earlier than planned?—but addressed himself to both of them.

"There's a *special party* going on upstairs. Know what I mean? And they're eating *sqot*. For some reason, Jonn doesn't seem to want you to know. If you want to try it, though, I've got some in our room. It's amazing. You take some salt—"

"No!"

Burk remembered, only too clearly, how Guardian Rebek'a had tried to force him to eat it; how it had pulsated in his hand, had *communed* with him; how she had told him that when you put salt on it, there was a biochemical reaction, and you would be eating its scream of pain, so to speak. Except that the scream would taste like a kiss.

"No, I don't want to eat it."

"Whatever you like. Though I thought you were the

one who wanted to see Lemnos and all its delights? Don't get me wrong! I'm looking forward to the trip very much. Guardian, it's going to be wonderful. We're so privileged that you chose us. But where we're going, there's not very much to see, is there? It's not as if we were going to Limbo-Limbo-Land. And *thank goodness* we aren't going there."

Burk turned his head away, so that Aylwin couldn't see him smile. That's what *you* think, my friend.

CHAPTER NINE
HOW *NOT* TO ORGANIZE
AN ORGY, PART TWO

THEY NEEDED AN EARLY START. That meant slipping away before the first breakfasts were served. After several nights of partying, few of the guests were likely to be breakfasting early, but some of the estate staff might. And they needed to be away from the estate before any new guests arrived from Lemnos City—well, one visitor in particular.

Outside, the night was cold. Zora hadn't risen yet, but the twin Kallipygian moons, Ogrob and Darnoc, gave a limited amount of light, so it was murky rather than dark. It was a different shuttle this time, cleaner and better suited for transporting passengers, but essentially the same model as the other one, and also with mechanical ignition, Milliya was pleased to note. Leyna stowed their bags efficiently in the luggage boot of the shuttle, and the four guests climbed in and strapped themselves into their safety-belts. The seating arrangements for passengers were similar to those on the transfer shuttle at the Gate—four seating berths in facing pairs—with the driver sitting in front, with her back to them.

Burk and Milliya made sure to take seats side by side. The other couple would have to stretch across to touch them, perhaps after unclipping their safety-belts first. That would discourage any touchy-feely stuff! But Aylwin and his wife were obviously still groggy. It would be a while before they were in the mood for foreplay, indeed, for *any* sort of play.

Burk was sleepy too. Milliya, on the other hand, was bright and frisky, bombarding Leyna with technical questions about the shuttle, how it operated, and what kind of things typically went wrong. She received brusque but what seemed to her to be honest answers. *Any* of this information could prove to be useful.

Suddenly Aylwin chipped in with a question too: "Are we going anywhere *dangerous*?" That must have been preying on his mind since the night before.

No. Master (that word again!) had given her clear instructions. Only safe places.

If those had been his words, it suggested strongly that there were places that *weren't* safe. But what did "safe" mean? Safe for whom? More specifically, Leyna had been instructed not to use the transit line between the estate and Lemnos City, so as to avoid meeting any incoming traffic head-on. They were therefore following a transit line that went off at a tangent to the main route. The countryside, they soon noticed, was dull and featureless even by Lemnian standards. There were no buildings to be seen, no jettisoned waste or litter, and in general no sign that this route was used very much.

There was no cultivated land either. The soil was gray-brown and of sandy consistency, though large areas were darker, as though the ground had been torched or the topsoil stripped away.

Milliya used Aylwin's question as a convenient opportunity to find out whether their driver was armed.

So, she posited: no weapons need to be taken on trips like this?

No.

That was both good and bad news.

Good, because they wouldn't have to deal with an extremely large person armed with a taser.

Bad, because now they would have to overwhelm Leyna physically (and how were they going to manage *that*?). Wresting the taser away from her, perhaps by means of a trick, and then threatening her with it would have been the easiest way to take charge.

Leyna probably didn't need a taser. Almost any bulky object would become a fearsome weapon if she swung it at you. And her fists were enormous, Burk had noticed. But her movements were slow—and perhaps her wits, too—and that could be to their advantage. However, the other passengers would need to keep out of their way.

They continued trundling across the Northern Lemnian Plain. The landcape was completely boring, and it could be said that the entertainment value of the 'safari' so far, the traveling part of it least, was close to zero. But they were not there for sightseeing. The entertainment program was going to be improvised, and three of the five people in the shuttle would be expecting it to start fairly soon, perhaps after lunch, even though one of them, Leyna, would not herself be taking part. Would she want to watch? Burk could hardly imagine that—and it gave him an idea. A *plan*. He whispered his thoughts to Milliya.

Midday came early on Lemnos. Zora throbbed, the air shimmered, and Aylwin and Keesha happily insisted on staying inside the air-conditioned shuttle for lunch instead of picnicking outside. That was all to the good, but Leyna seemed annoyed.

She had brought the craft to a halt a stone's throw away from a clump of bedraggled-looking bushes. There was a similar clump of vegetation a little further on. The natural beauties of Lemnos had been quite a disappointment so far! Burk saw how cleverly Leyna had set it up. Assuming that they were already outside, picnicking, slurping Goro-nut whiskey and flirting with each other more and more aggressively, once the *serious stuff* started each couple would then have a cosy, secluded love-nest to go to. Leyna must have gathered experience on earlier pleasure trips of this kind. Perhaps she knew this spot, and always brought her amorous passengers here? While they were sporting in the bushes, Leyna could have a comfortable nap back in the shuttle.

After they had eaten, it was Aylwin who made the first move.

"The banana custard was delicious, wasn't it? But I

really had something else in mind for dessert."

"Something tasty," his wife said, "and I know just where it is!"

Upon which she thrust her hand between Burk's thighs and seized hold of the dessert in question.

Burk gasped, Milliya blinked and Leyna looked away.

"Are we going to party or not? I'm *Keesha*, by the way. In case you'd forgotten."

"Pleased to meet you, Keesha," Burk said, with as much aplomb as he could muster. It's hard to stay cool when you're having your parts massaged—*kneaded* would be a better word—by an attractive stranger.

With that the pairings were presumably established, at least for the first round, and Aylwin seemed delighted with the arrangements. He gave Milliya a dewy-eyed look. "My dear."

Keesha paid no attention to him. "You and I could take a little walk, Mr. Burk? Thataway, into the woods? Because I think my husband may want the air-conditioning! You don't mind, do you?"

"Not at all. He told us a few things at the Gate of Lemnos, so we've brought along some toys." Burk nodded towards the back of the shuttle, where the hold was located.

Only then did she release her grip.

"Clever boy. But leave some for my husband!"

Leyna opened the hold for him, and Burk brought out the bundles of ropes, as well as cushions and a light mattress for the floor of the shuttle. After all, Aylwin wouldn't want to get any *unintentional* bruises.

"We have some toys, too, in the pink bag. But I'll leave them here with you, darling, so that you can get some proper *Guardian discipline*."

She hesitated. "Leyna, sweetheart—"

Leyna was still looking away from them.

"—we haven't spoken about whether you'd like to.... You know? You could come with us...."

Keesha can scarcely have expected the estate manager to say yes, Burk thought, but what if she *had*? That would have been awkward.

"Have good time. I'll sleep." Leyna climbed out of the shuttle and marched off in the direction of the more distant clump of bushes.

So far, so good. Excellent, in fact.

Burk picked up half the ropes and followed Keesha over to the clump of vegetation. Her reference to "the woods" may have been ironic, but when they slipped between the bushes Burk discovered to his surprise that inside there was a low indentation covered with moss of some kind, not *sqot* of course, and that the foliage met above their heads to create a natural chamber. The moss was comfortably soft under their feet, and the air inside the bushes pleasantly cool.

"A proper little love-nest, Mr. Burk, don't you think?"

Keesha was already stripping.

If their plan was to succeed, Burk and Milliya must now time what they were doing very carefully. But Keesha was going too fast! At this rate, Burk would soon have to move from the theoretical to the practical, which was clearly what she wanted. The prospect was not entirely unappealing. She slipped out of the last of her clothes.

"Do you like what you see?"

Keesha had a luscious, shapely body, far more womanly than Milliya's. She grabbed at him, and this time it was *his* hand that went between *her* thighs, although it was she who placed it there. She was ready for him, he noticed.

"Now listen. I intend to enjoy this, Mr. Burk, and so will you, but we have to do it *my* way. At *my* speed. I'll show you *what* to do, and *when*. Okay?" He nodded. "Why don't you make yourself more comfortable?"

She released his hand. Burk began removing his clothes, as slowly as possible, folding them precisely and placing them in a neat little pile. Something he never did at home!

Keesha snorted impatiently. "Oh, my stallion, you just can't wait, can you?"

"You have *your* way of doing things, as you say, and that's fine with me. But I have *my* little habits, too. And we have plenty of time, don't we?" (Which wasn't true, though Keesha didn't know that.)

She laughed. "Well, there's *one* part of you that wants to get on with it!"

Looking down, he realized to his great embarrassment that she was right.

"Mr. Burk, what was it that my husband told you about our...*preferences*? Specifically, now!"

"Oh, bondage? Control? That's why I brought along the ropes. And he said that you went in for *punishment* and stuff."

She smiled. "That's just my dear husband. Not me. He needs a taste of discipline to perk up his interest. From a man or a woman. He's quite hoping that *you'll* do him the honor before this trip is over. You brought ropes. We brought canes and, er, other items."

Burk's horror was genuine.

"No cause for alarm, Mr Burk! Just the discipline part, that's all. After that his needs are boringly conventional. *Hetero*, as they used to say."

"Oh, I don't think I could."

"Why not? It's easy enough. You don't need to hurt him. Use your hand if you like. Smack his flabby buns for him! Warm him up for the main course!"

"Well, I've never done anything like that...."

"You're a proper virgin, aren't you? Here, get down, I'll show you how."

"No!" Then he lowered his voice. "Sorry. You're very attractive. But being hit—even by you!—that would be a big turn-off for me."

"So you always have to be on top? How conventional! Okay, then *you* give *me* a good smacking! Take me over your lap...."

"No. I wouldn't do that with him. That would be much too...you know—"

"—gay? Alright, then how about this?"

She lay on the ground on her stomach, presenting her delightful backside for his attention.

"Go on, touch them. Stroke them. More! Hmm. Yes, that's nice. Slip your hand between my legs a bit—"

"No."

"Because you wouldn't do that with him, right?" She sighed. "Boy, you've got a lot to learn. Now: smack me!"

He obliged. Her bottom quivered deliciously.

"And again! Keep going! Oh, I could learn to enjoy this."

Burk already was enjoying it. Her skin had a lovely satiny texture, and seemed to come alive as he smacked her. But then he stopped.

"What's wrong, Mr. Burk? You were just getting into your rhythm."

"Doesn't he expect to be tied up as well? I don't think I know how to do that."

"True. You're right. Okay. I'll show you. I'll tie you up, and then I'll give *your* bottom a working over."

"No, *I* need to learn how to do it. Look, Keesha, if I try to tie you up, can you tell me if I'm doing it right?"

"Well hurry up. I want some action before our lovely driver wakes up and tells us it's time to go."

Keesha rolled over onto her back. Burk fetched the ropes and did a surprisingly competent job in tying her up—Milliya had instructed him well. While he was working he asked her for advice or comments.

"You're actually pretty good at this, Mr. Burk. Are you sure you haven't done it before? If you hadn't tied my legs together quite so tightly, I would say: what about a quick one right now? While I'm at your mercy?"

"Now aren't you two just having fun?"

Milliya was there. And unlike them, she was fully clothed. Keesha smiled up at her.

"What have you done with my dear husband, Guardian? I hope he's getting his money's worth!"

"I left him to stew for a bit. I heard no complaints."

"Perhaps you'd care to join us? Your boyfriend was about to administer further punishment. You may have some rare skill, some subtle Guardian refinement, that we don't know about? I promise to reward you! You'll be quite surprised—"

Burk had never seen Milliya move so fast. She stuffed something deep into Keesha's open mouth and, as Keesha spluttered and tried to spit it out, quickly wrapped a strip of cloth around her head and tied it at the back.

"No, *you'll* be surprised, my dear." She stepped back and surveyed Keesha's bound, naked body. "You were enjoying this, weren't you, Burk? A bit too much, I would say. She's a good-looking woman, I have to admit. Better figure than mine, if it's tits that you want. And *much* better looking than her husband, that's for sure."

She checked the ropes and the knots.

"The ropes are good. Well done, I'll make a Guardian of you yet! Now, come and admire *my* handiwork. And then we must go, before Leyna wakes up. Oh, one last thing: those clothes of hers. Find her personal communicator. *That* goes with *us*."

As Burk slipped out through the bushes he turned

and looked back at Keesha, who was wriggling in the most inviting way. "I'm sorry!" he said. Which could have meant several things....

CHAPTER TEN
THE OTHER SIDE

AYLWIN, NAKED, BOUND AND GAGGED, was a far less attractive sight than Keesha had been. Burk looked away in embarrassment.

"You could at least admire my knots." Aylwin had been trussed up most professionally. "I praised yours, didn't I?"

Burk didn't feel happy about what they were doing.

"Don't be sentimental," Milliya said. "You know what's at stake here."

She told him to help her carry Aylwin out of the shuttle. They placed him well to one side of the craft, so that he wouldn't be injured when they set off, and left him some of the provisions, and the two bags that he and Keesha had brought with them, though only after Milliya had removed his personal communicator.

"If she's SurPop, as I'm guessing, Leyna hasn't got one. She would use the communicator in the shuttle. But if she *has* got one, we're in trouble. Now: hurry!"

The mechanical ignition key was not to be found. Leyna had taken it with her.

"Can you start it?"

"What do you think they teach us in the Guardians? Paper-folding? Watch, and *don't* learn. This is highly illegal."

Burk couldn't quite see what Milliya did, but it was just as well that it worked first time because, as the ignition began to roar, and the shuttle started to throb, they saw Leyna stumbling sleepily out of the bushes.

"Is my passenger strapped in? Then off we go!"

They sped off from the scene of the crime, the shuttle whipping up a mass of gray-brown dust particles from the surface before Milliya slowed the craft down to a normal cruising speed. Even without looking at the navigation console, Burk could see from the few familiar patches of vegetation and the position of Zora in the sky that they were heading back down the same route they had taken a few hours earlier.

"Let them think that we're going back to the estate! If Leyna *has* got a communicator with her, she'll tell them that we freaked out. You know, the fun and games turned sour, we quarreled, or we've gone for a joy-ride, something like that?"

"And what if she *hasn't* got a communicator with her?"

"Well, darling, what do *you* think? First of all, she'll find our two trussed-up chickens and have to untie them."

Burk had in real life never seen a trussed-up chicken—on Terra, AdPops didn't eat meat very often—but he couldn't help laughing at the thought of Leyna fumbling to release the two naked bondage victims, most likely looking away in disgust while she did so.

"Then they'll have a very...long...walk. Our friend Aylwin is not a tough guy. He won't let Leyna leave him and Keesha all on their own out in the desert, and he won't want to move until it cools down. When they *do* set off, they won't be going anywhere fast: he'll slow the two women down. And they'll stop anyway when it gets dark."

"They've got provisions...."

"He and Keesha would be lost, but Leyna will know how to find her way, just following the direction receivers, at least in daylight. And once they hit a main transit route they might get picked up by a passing shuttle."

"Good that we left them their clothes!" They both laughed.

"And now," said Milliya, "it's time to turn this baby north-north-east. We can use the navigation system. The settlers can't track us, they don't have that kind of equipment. *We hope.*"

"But the Government does. Guardian Sousanna...."

"Yes. She's looking for us. But she's not looking for this shuttle, is she? Not yet. And the settlers won't willingly give her that information. I think we'll have a day or two to look at the Other Side. After that, though, we'll have to take our chances."

As it grew dark, Burk noticed how the glow from distant estates or farms was still faintly visible. They must light them up like wedding cakes in the evening, he thought, as if they were trying to raise a protest against loneliness, out here on the edge of the known universe. The gradual disappearance of these dim lights on the horizon was in fact the first indication that they were now probably on the Other Side.

They traveled on for another hour, until Milliya began to yawn and stretch. She brought the shuttle to a halt.

"Let's take a break. I want to move my legs. After that, we ought to sleep for a few hours."

When she powered down the shuttle, Milliya also switched off the lights.

"Is that wise? It's very dark out there!"

"Trust me."

They climbed down onto the surface. Milliya dropped to her knees and started feeling and examining the soil. Burk did the same, without knowing what he was supposed to be looking for.

"Look, there!"

Burk couldn't see anything.

"There. In the middle distance. Can't you see that the ground is *glowing*?"

"Yes, very faintly. More like: shimmering."

"They cleared *sqot* from here. Maybe it did something to the ground? Look, it's topsoil, it's not rock."

"Strange. Maybe it's a chemical reaction? It might be crystals causing the effect. We should take samples back with us."

Milliya laughed cynically. "*If* we get back."

Now that Burk had noticed it, he saw that the surface

all around them, from the shuttle to the horizon, was gleaming and shimmering. The night was warm.

"I want to sleep outside! Don't you?"

"Are you sure?"

It was unusual for Burk to be the daring one, and for Milliya to be cautious. But he pointed out to her that there were no wild animals on Lemnos—there weren't even very many left on Terra—and that no-one would be sneaking around on foot in the middle of the night, in the middle of nowhere. If a shuttle full of settlers or Guardians came along, they'd see it and hear it if they were awake; and if they were asleep, it wouldn't matter whether they were inside the shuttle or outside.

"But if you want we can take turns to keep watch. I'll go first if you like—it's such a beautiful night."

"Okay. I'll fetch some blankets and cushions."

But she didn't move. They were still both on their knees, facing each other. Milliya tilted her head, in the way that he loved so much.

"Are you thinking what I'm thinking?"

"I don't know. I'm not a Guardian. I wasn't trained to think like one."

"So what *are* you thinking?"

"Oh, forbidden thoughts. Something I'd like to do. With a Guardian. Strictly against the rules, of course. I'm only AdPop, you know."

"I wonder what that might be? You're a man of action, as we saw this afternoon. With the lovely Keesha."

"Nothing happened."

"But you *wanted* something to happen, didn't you?"

"Yes, but with you."

"Oh, so you want to strip a Guardian naked, tie her up, smack her bottom, and then give her a good rogering?"

"I wouldn't tie you up, but as for the rest: yes, definitely!"

"So you'd smack my bottom?"

"Yes. If you gave me permission...."

Instead of answering, Milliya kissed him. She began undoing his clothes.

"You do it," she said huskily. "We don't need blankets, do we?"

He was undressed before she was. As she slipped off her top he took one of her breasts in his hand, then leant forward and kissed the nipple, gently sucking and biting at it. He repeated it with the other breast. She sighed, and pulled him down on top of her, kissing him and pushing her tongue into his mouth. As they kissed, his groin rubbed into hers. She was still half-dressed.

"Wait," she said.

He lifted himself off her body. Raising her bottom slightly off the ground, she pulled with both hands at the trouser pants and knickers that she was wearing, dragging them down over her hips and then kicking them aside. It was dark, but Burk could see the neatly trimmed hair on her mound, and a suggestion of the delights below. She opened her thighs in invitation.

"Come," she whispered. "And you can smack me afterwards, if you still want to."

He kissed what she was offering him, but they were

both too eager to want to spend time on foreplay. He entered her, and she groaned and wrapped her legs around him.

"You go on top," he said, remembering that there was no blanket to protect her skin from the ground. "Roll with me."

And in one rolling movement they changed positions without him having to withdraw from her body. But their lovemaking was soon over. The sight of her breasts hanging down over him excited Burk so much that he came almost immediately, in an uncontrollable burst of passion. Did Milliya climax as well? He couldn't be sure, but he saw how she looked away from him when his moment came, before slumping down onto him with a shuddering of her own body.

She lay on his chest, very still, listening to his heart. Neither of them said a word.

It had been good. Not perfect, though. It might be the last time. If they survived, and got back to Lemnos City, and even to Terra, it would be difficult for them to stay together, let alone to get married. And did she really want him? She had been holding something back. She couldn't look at him when he climaxed.

He had made love to her honestly, thinking only of her. Not a single thought of Keesha, not a single image of her naked body, had entered his mind. *Now* they did so, but it wasn't Keesha that he wanted, it was still Milliya, and only her.

He should let her sleep, and take the "first watch" as agreed, but the way she was lying on him, weighing down on him as if she wanted to push herself into him through his skin, was having an arousing effect, and he felt himself begin to stiffen again. Milliya seemed to be aware of this too.

Or of something else.

"Don't move," she whispered urgently. "Keep still! We're not alone."

"What do you mean?"

"Shhh."

Strangely, she didn't seem to be frightened. He didn't dare to look properly, but what was there to see? There was no shuttle, except their own. There were no figures of Guardians or settler thugs looming up out of the darkness. There were no alien monsters, no Outsiders waiting to disembowel them.

"Take your hands off my backside, Mr. Burk. And put them on the ground, very slowly."

Burk did as she asked. At first he didn't notice anything, but then he felt a gentle rubbing, warm and just a little moist. A pulsating that was somehow familiar.

Now he looked. It was up against his naked body on all sides, and on all sides it stretched away into the darkness as far as he could see. It gleamed and glowed more strongly than the soil had done. It was what they had come to see: *sqot.*

"What do we do?"

Outwardly she was calm, but there was an untypical tremor of fear in Milliya's voice, he thought. It was easier for him to relax. He was lying on his back; she was lying on top of him.

"Don't panic."

That almost did the trick. She was quite annoyed with him.

"Darling, I – NEVER – EVER – PANIC. Okay? You're the big baby here, remember? But what do we *do*?"

"It reads our emotions. Maybe our thoughts, too. The pulsating and the glowing: that's communication. Transmission. Do you mean it any harm? Do you have any bad emotions? We're here to help it, aren't we?"

"Yes, we are." She seemed calmer now.

He had said "it", but was it an "it" or a they"? It was a *collective being*—that much he had learnt about *sqot*—or it was a *collective of beings*, with individualities that shifted, formed and re-formed according to what was needed for the greater good.

Sqot had helped them to overcome Guardian Rebek'a in a mysterious way that Burk still couldn't fathom. On the *Starstretcher*, Burk had held *sqot* in his hand. He had communed with it. He had felt its goodness, and kindness. Or had he sensed *sqot* feeling *his* goodness, and *his* kindness, and transmitting that discovery to its collective consciousness?

Scribe Jacoob had taken the little box of *sqot* from the *Starstretcher* with him. Had he been able to smuggle it past the Gate? *Sqot* would have helped him! He had seen how it could change its shape or position, how it could sense what needed to be done, and intervene in dangerous situations. Jacoob would have released it back on the surface of Lemnos, but here on the Other

Side they were many leagues away from where that could have been.

Burk sensed that this *sqot* knew him, and knew about what had happened on the *Starstretcher*. Yet how could that be? It could read emotions, but could it also read *thoughts*, if they too were tinged with emotion?

Most of all—they were now surrounded by *sqot*: what did it want from them?

"Milliya, we have nothing to fear. It's come to meet us. It means us no harm."

"It's *touching* me, Burk. It's moving over my body."

"Let it. It wants to know you. It's come a long way to find us."

He felt that it was touching every part of his body. But so was Milliya. Her skin was alive against his, touching all his limbs, warming and stroking his nerve-endings. Her eyes were looking deep into his, just as Keesha's had done—but suddenly, strangely, the thought of Keesha was eradicated from his consciousness and it was Milliya's eyes and hers only that were interlocked with his. Though he had no sense of her changing position, he was now inside her. Or was she around *him*, or were they twined together like the branches of fast-growing vegetation, moving in and out of and between each other?

They had been on the ground, but now they seemed to be floating above it. The movement began—a movement of their conjoined bodies that should have been like a thrusting piston, he had enough clear-headed consciousness to know that that was what it should have been, but instead it was more like a *flowing* that was happening between them.

Now he could see into Milliya, saw extremely clearly her frightened childhood, saw her making herself better, cleverer, and more successful in order to cover over those wounds, saw Rebek'a giving her more knowledge and outward self-confidence, but sucking at her insecurity in their own relationship. He saw Milliya looking deep into *him*. He didn't need to know what she was seeing. Her eyes were wide open, he knew what he was, and so he also knew what Milliya would find.

The pleasure was there too, building slowly and exquisitely from the contact of sensitive membranes, like the opening up of a long succession of tiny little petals. He knew that Milliya was still on top of him, and that his back should be rubbing itself into the gray-brown dirt of the planet and into *sqot*, but instead they floated, their bodies being passed along a chain of trusting hands, higher and faster, with no feeling that they could possibly fall, and, as the pleasure grew, with everything around them dissolving into a synesthetic blur of touch and color and smell and sound until the universe simply...melted.

They lay there exhausted. Burk moved her gently down, so that they were now side by side. Above their heads, Ogrob and Darnoc, the famous Kallipygian moons of Lemnos, glowed in the night sky. *Sqot* was nowhere to be seen.

"What *was* that, Burk?" Her eyes flashed as she

turned her head towards him. "What was it?

"I think that may have been a present, from *sqot* to you and me," Burk said. "A *thank you note*."

CHAPTER ELEVEN
THERE ARE PLACES
YOU SHOULDN'T GO

THERE WAS STILL *SQOT* ON LEMNOS. It had come to *them*, and now it was gone. Where it had been, the surface had a different color and texture, and glowed. As the light returned, the glow disappeared, but the other changes remained.

"You say that that was a present?"

Milliya had prepared them breakfast, although this was a duty that an AdPop would normally perform for a Guardian, and not the other way round.

"For what we did on the *Starstretcher*? And for Jacoob taking that other *sqot* and releasing it on the surface? This *sqot* must have found out about the other *sqot*—"

"No, Milliya, there is no 'this' or 'the other' with *sqot*. It's just...*sqot*. But I can't explain it."

"So *sqot* is our friend?"

"Perhaps. I felt it was calling to me. Maybe it wants us to do something for it. Maybe it *needs* us. We should move on. There is something else here. Something that *sqot* wants us to see."

"Strange. I sense that too."

"This planet belongs to *sqot*, not to the settlers. *Sqot* is willing to share, but the settlers aren't."

While Burk cleared up the remains of their breakfast, Milliya took some soil samples. When she started up the shuttle, this time she showed Burk how to do it.

"Just in case anything happens to me."

He assured her that he would stay with her.

"Okay, let me rephrase that. Just in case anything *terminal* happens to me, and if we have recordings on my communicator that the Terran Empire urgently needs to know about."

They continued in the same direction, through a similar cheerless landscape as before. After about an hour, the terrain began to change. The surface was rough, as if it had been churned up. Using hand controls, Milliya had to maneuver the shuttle between mounds, almost small hills, of dust, pebbles and soil. Some of them looked recent. She slowed the craft down considerably. Not only was there the danger of ramming into one of the mounds—which wouldn't destroy the shuttle, though the jet-drives might become clogged up with debris—there was the possibility that, behind one of them, there might *be* something, or even someone. What they saw around them looked far more like the work of human beings (or of Outsiders, as Burk gloomily suggested) than a natural feature of the topography of Lemnos.

Even at very slow speed, they could so easily have run straight into whoever was creating those mounds.

Fortunately, Milliya was now wide-awake, and spotted it immediately. She jammed on the shuttle's braking mechanism.

"Look! There, over to the left. *Smoke!*"

Sure enough, there was a modest wisp of smoke visible above a group of mounds some considerable distance away. It was almost on the horizon, Burk thought, but Milliya insisted that they leave the shuttle and approach whatever it was on foot. That proved to be a wise decision: the smoke was much closer than Burk had realized (and, Lemnos being smaller than Terra, the horizon was in any case always much nearer than you thought).

They walked, crept, and finally crawled to as close as they dared to go, then peered carefully round the side of an obviously very recent mound of soil and small stones. (Not over the top, Milliya had told him: if anyone's looking, that's where their eyes are more likely to be fixed; also, you're less likely to set off a mini-avalanche at the *side* of a pile of earth than at the *top*. Okay, Burk said, I'm not stupid. And don't say "earth"—this is Lemnos, not Terra.)

What they had expected to see was some nasty settlers stripping and burning off *sqot*. Milliya had her personal communicator with her, to record just such a scene. Switching it on would be dangerous—there was a real chance that the Government tracking station at Lemnos City would pick it up, or a satellite—but if they could avoid meeting up with Guardian Rebek'a or any of her settler friends, if they could evade capture, arrest or worse at the hands of Government agents, if they could get back to Terra, whatever material they could show to a commission of enquiry might save *sqot*, and change the history of the universe.

That is what they had expected to see, but it wasn't what they saw.

Nothing was being burnt. The smoke came from an ancient-looking excavator with an old-fashioned engine. The machine was stripping off not *sqot*, but topsoil—the same kind of topsoil, with an unusual color and texture, that they had seen elsewhere on Lemnos too.

"What are they doing? Are they *mining*?"

The excavator seemed to be extracting some element or other from the soil and depositing the rest in a heap to one side.

"Burk, use your brain! What could they possibly be mining here? And why are they using such an antique piece of machinery to do it? It's even got an operator. This isn't authorized. Burk, this is *illegal*."

The man who was operating the excavator was wearing protective glasses and some kind of working overalls, but standing nearby was a woman who looked more like a thug than a mining engineer. She wore boots, and was dressed in a black, semi-military outfit, with a taser and a machete hanging from her belt.

"I know that one," Milliya said. "She's on our Guardian Wanted List. She is *bad, bad news*."

"Why the machete?" Burk wished that they had picked up a taser somewhere along the way.

Milliya ignored his question. She was already switching on her personal communicator to record the scene.

"Look over there: beyond the excavator, behind what they've just piled up."

"I can't see anything. You can see better through the communicator."

"Look *carefully*."

Then Burk saw it. Peeping out from behind the mounds of soil was the top of a shuttle.

"We need to take a good look at that, Mr. Burk. People can change their clothes so that you don't know who they are, but a shuttle? That will tell us who we're dealing with here."

The problem was that there was no direct way to get closer to the craft without being seen, so they would have to take the long way round. And every step would take them further away from their own shuttle, and safety.

"If we're spotted, those two will get to our shuttle before we can. And she's armed." (And she looks pretty nasty, too, Burk thought.)

"Then we don't *get* spotted."

Milliya checked him over for bright objects that might catch the light of Zora and draw attention to them. He had to take off his belt, which had a shiny buckle. She herself slipped the communicator inside her sleeve. She explained to Burk how "creeping unnoticed" was taught to Guardians.

She laughed. "You do realize what you're getting

here? A crash course in Guardian basics! When we get back, how do you fancy joining the Guardians?"

The long way round proved to be just that. Several times, when there were no convenient little hillocks to hide behind, they had to crawl over flat ground like snakes. Eventually they reached a vantage point beyond the excavator from which they could view the whole scene.

It wasn't a shuttle; it was *two*. Milliya sucked in her breath. Then she began recording.

One of the shuttles was an elderly, very dirty, freight transporter. Two men and a woman, dressed and armed like the woman near the excavator, were stowing crates on board the craft. Or rather: the two men were stowing the crates, while the woman supervised them. The woman suddenly walked away, and disappeared behind the shuttle.

The other craft was much smaller, and of a design that Burk had never seen before.

Near to the shuttles there was a row of tents, with signs of an extinguished campfire. A short distance behind was an area that was plainly being used as a latrine.

He looked at Milliya.

"That's enough. Switch it off now."

"I couldn't get their faces properly. And the woman's gone off somewhere."

"No, we've got what we need. It's dangerous to leave it switched on for so long."

She switched off the communicator.

"Okay, it's done. You take the thing." She handed it to him. "If a tracker has picked us up, so be it. If they send someone, take the shuttle, and *go*. Go as fast as you can! I'll try and distract them. And what they find here will keep them busy, too."

"What do you mean by that? What *will* they find?"

"*That*, Mr. Burk," and she pointed to the smaller of the shuttles, "is a transporter for moving people between the surface and the Gate of Lemnos. Or directly to an orbiting space-craft. In other words, it's a transit vehicle—an expensive little item. Granted it's an old design. These models were collected and replaced years ago. Officially, they were destroyed. But obviously someone made other arrangements."

"Do you mean: the Government?"

"No. Does this look like a Guardian operation to you? We haven't really got time for this, but that over there," and she pointed to the other shuttle, "is an old freight carrier. A *very* old one. They're loading it with something that they extract from the soil here. Funny-colored soil, and we've seen it before...."

"It's soil from where *sqot* used to be!"

"Well done! Did Mrs. Burk ever realize that you were leadership material? Now, can we go?"

"And these are Jonn's settler friends? And Guardian Rebek'a's?"

"Yes and no. They've got a transit, an illegal one, so they must have a space-craft too, also illegal. Mr. Burk, I hate to say this, but: please meet the Outsiders!"

It took a moment for it to sink in.

"What do they need machetes for?"

She smiled. "Oh, for mutilating, and disemboweling. It's what they do."

He gave her back the communicator.

"Take it. We stay together, Milliya. *Whatever* happens."

CHAPTER TWELVE
SEVERAL DISTINCTLY
DIFFERENT VIEWPOINTS

THE RETURN JOURNEY took a very long time. They had to wait endlessly while the man operating the excavator drove it to and fro while he quarreled with his lady colleague. Milliya used the opportunity to take more soil samples.

They could have been arguing about which stretch of ground to do next, or in which order different stretches should be done. Burk and Milliya were terrified that they might decide to drive over to look at a new area close to where their shuttle was parked, and might suddenly see it. Without the shuttle, without weapons and without food, they would be hopelessly lost.

After the couple with the excavator had finally reached an agreement and started to work on a new patch of soil, Burk and Milliya began the journey back, taking the same route, crawling and creeping again, but with a greater sense of urgency. It seemed to take forever, and Burk was certain that they'd made enough noise both to wake the dead and to alarm the living.

"I must start it gently," Milliya said, after they had

reached the shuttle. "Once we get moving, they'll never catch us in that old transporter."

"Quite right, princess! But now they won't need to, will they?"

They turned around fast. It was Guardian Rebek'a, not in Guardian uniform but dressed (and armed) like the others they had seen. Except that she was holding her taser, and had it trained on them.

"Move away from the shuttle, but stay close together. I'm good, but I can't taser both of you at the same time. So if you move too far apart I'll have to maim one of you."

Despite her threatening size, she was physically attractive. The overall effect was spoiled, however, by the Medusa gaze that she so often fixed on people. Now, however, she switched to a different expression—the grin of a professional torturer satisfied with the day's results.

"I trained you well, Milliya. You were always hard to track. But today you made too much noise. Your pedophile lover boy here—what's his name: Jerk? Prat? *Burk*, that was it!—he makes more noise than a herd of AdPops at a free buffet. To think you gave *me* up for *him*! That is not very flattering, my dear."

"You know that he's not a pedophile. That was a set-up. He's a decent human being. And he's capable of love—unlike you!"

Burk couldn't believe his ears, but Guardian Rebek'a was not impressed.

"What is he: SurPop? AdPop? And he's a *man*!" Her

voice hardened. "You know, I didn't much appreciate being dumped in a waste bin. I think I'll maim him just for fun...."

"It wasn't *his* idea! He refused to kill you. You owe him your life!"

"I know what I owe, and everyone will get what they deserve. I don't know whose idea it was with the waste bin. I *do* know who made special arrangements to get me killed, and when I meet the creepy little hunchback I'll take my time with him, oh yes. But what do I do with *you*?"

"I'm sorry about what happened on the *Starstretcher*, but you tried to separate us, didn't you? People in love do illogical things sometimes, don't they? The hunchback took advantage of us. We didn't intend you to come to harm!"

Burk had never heard Milliya talk like this. He had to admire what she was trying to do, but would her former lover be convinced?

"Oh, you didn't?"

"No. And we've done what you wanted, Rebek'a. We've collected the information that you need."

"So Jonn told me, when I eventually managed to reach him. I've been having a rough time here on Lemnos, as you may have gathered. People have been asking awkward questions. My papers have gone astray. Not to worry—these are only temporary problems. So: where is this information then?"

Milliya reached inside her top and fumbled for something.

"Here, it's on this. On my personal communicator."

"Good. Now listen carefully. I want you to throw it to me, princess, so that I can catch it with my other hand without taking my eyes off you. The same way we practiced it in Guardian training. Get it right, and I *won't* shoot him. Even if I do, he might be lucky: I can't remember what setting my taser is on: 'Low'? 'Medium'? 'Maximum Sedation'? I honestly don't know, and I'm not going to check it now. I just don't recommend taking a gamble on it. There's a big difference between pain and death. But you're not a gambling man, are you, Mr. Burk? No, I thought not."

"Here."

In a gentle arc, Milliya threw the communicator across to Guardian Rebek'a, who caught it with her free hand.

"Well done! Just as I taught you."

In the distance was the sound of a shuttle.

"Good. My colleagues will be here in a moment. I said I'd go on ahead and deal with it. As I *am* dealing with it. I told them to clear out the crates and make some room in the back. For your bodies. But now that I have this"—she held up the communicator—"I don't need to kill you. We'll leave you somewhere out here to die. And if by chance you are found, it's the word of two Wanted Persons, and no evidence, against the word of a senior Guardian. You see, princess? This is now *me* being nice to *you*."

She held up the communicator.

"Is there anything else on this?" She gave them the

torturer's grin once more. "Dirty, private stuff? Jonn said that you'd been having fun at the estate. Partying. Going on a 'sex safari'. Where is the other couple, by the way? Never mind! Who cares? I'll have to delete the other things, but before I do that I'll watch everything once. It'll remind me of the fun that *we* used to have together. Stuff that Burk wouldn't understand. Things that *girls* do. *Sophisticated* girls."

"Rebek'a, I'll stay with you if you let him go."

"No!"

"How romantic! How noble! But I wonder: would he sacrifice himself for *you*?"

A shuttle came to a noisy halt some way behind her, and slightly to the side, so as not to throw up too much dust.

"And isn't it interesting? We have three distinctly different viewpoints here. Although only one of them truly counts: *mine.*"

"Four viewpoints, I think you'll find."

Guardian Rebek'a spun round. Her fellow Guardian, Sousanna, had climbed quietly out of her own shuttle and was now facing her, her taser in her hand.

"Oh, it's bloody Golden Girl Sousanna! You're all I need! What have you done with my friends?"

"They were *un*friendly, so I tasered them to sleep. But only to sleep—"

"All of them? *That's* why you didn't shoot me in the back while you had the chance. Your taser is still recharging. Well, you won't get another opportunity."

The two Guardians faced each other, tasers drawn.

It was like a scene from one of those silly old twentieth-century entertainments called "Westerns", Burk thought.

"No, Guardian, my job is to investigate people, not to execute them. Your behavior on the *Starstretcher* was erratic, and so is your behavior now, but have you done anything to warrant execution? Also, I would never shoot someone in the back. I don't even have a warrant for your arrest."

At that moment, she looked as majestic as Guardian Rebek'a looked fearsome.

"You're too good to be true!"

Pallas Athene ignored that remark. "Why were you holding these two at taser point? And what is that in your other hand?"

"Just my personal communicator."

"I didn't realize that you still had one. Put it slowly back in your pocket. I assume that you haven't got a second taser hidden there? It's not a standard Guardian uniform that you're wearing, is it?"

"Don't be childish." She slipped Milliya's communicator into her jacket pocket. "You know that I left everything on the *Starstretcher.*"

"Yes, including your official documentation. So be polite to me. Guardian Mykel, the Commander of the *Starstretcher*, has made a Form 85a Complaint about your behavior. You should be walking on eggshells here. I was sent to Lemnos to investigate conditions on the planet. I find you on the Other Side, as they call it, in dubious company. What *are* you doing here,

Rebek'a, may I ask?"

Guardian Rebeka's neck bulged with anger. She leveled the taser at her colleague.

"I don't like your tone, Miss High-and-Mighty! And don't forget that I outrank you, with or without documentation. If you want to know what I was doing, I was visiting some old acquaintances who work out here, and taking soil samples for potential farmers and settlers. I apprehended two Wanted Persons. I'm doing your job for you! *You're* Crime and Security, aren't you? I'm in the Ideology Section. You should be *thanking* me, not waving a taser in my face!"

Guardian Sousanna had the advantage that she could see, and address, Burk and Milliya without turning.

"Guardian Milliya. AdPop John Burk. It is my duty to take you into custody to answer various charges made against you."

"And if we don't want to be taken?"

Guardian Rebek'a snorted with delight.

"You pompous cow! See how seriously our little friends take you? And quite right too!"

"I said: it's my *duty.* I didn't say: it's my *priority.* There are other Guardians who can chase you and arrest you. I wasn't sent to Lemnos to do that." In a different tone, she continued: "Guardian Milliya, will you give me your solemn word that you and AdPop John Burk will in the foreseeable future present yourselves to my department to answer these charges?"

Burk and Milliya looked at each other. Milliya's lips silently formed the word "yes".

"Okay, we agree."

"John Burk: you as well?" He nodded. "Then you can go. In your case, Mr. Burk, I expect the most serious matter, the pedophile charge, to be dropped. That will certainly be my recommendation."

"So you're just letting them go? *Very* professional! Why don't you shoot them?"

"Because they're not threatening me, Guardian; but you *are*. Your taser is pointing at me, and if I aim at *them* you might shoot me. So: lower your taser, place it on the ground, move away from it, and I might then consider arresting them."

But Burk and Milliya were already in the shuttle, and Milliya was working on the ignition.

"And if I turn round and taser them, what will you do?"

"I won't shoot you in the back. Well, *probably* not. But you're too late—they'll be gone in a moment. And why should you taser them anyway? Have they harmed you? Are they a danger to you?"

Guardian Rebek'a could feel Milliya's communicator in her pocket, pressing slightly against her side. She smiled.

"No, of course not. They can tell stories about me, but that's all. They think I'm the big bad wolf that's been eating all the *sqot*. But do you see any *sqot* around here? I don't. I say that it's the Government, and that there are people who can prove that. You're just here to do a cover-up."

"I'm here to find out the truth."

"Maybe I can help you there. I know a lot of the settlers...."

"Your settler friends at the big estate were not very helpful."

"With a recommendation from me it would have been *so much easier*—"

Guardian Sousanna wasn't sure whether that was meant ironically.

"—but they did send you here, didn't they? They knew that our friends were curious about the Other Side. And so we were lucky enough to bump into each other!"

"It wasn't luck. She switched on her personal communicator, and we tracked it."

"Ah, that was a mistake, wasn't it, Guardian? But I have to ask: why haven't you confiscated the thing? It might have important data on it! But it's gone now."

"How was I supposed to confiscate anything with you waving a taser at me?"

"And what about *your* taser?"

"I'm Crime and Security, I'm allowed to wave it!"

This time they both laughed.

"So what do we do now? What do you suggest? I outrank you, so I propose that you lower your taser and leave. My friends will be waking up soon, and they might be feeling resentful."

"I set my taser to 'MEDIUM', so your friends won't be waking up any time soon. As for your status—that may have been suspended. Guardian Mykel wasn't too happy about your behavior. And there is a shuttle with

Security Guardians now on its way from Lemnos City. I just happened to be in the vicinity, so I got here first. Do you play chess? You're in check! I propose that *you* lower your weapon, and that you come with me to answer questions."

"My friends will be out of it for a bit longer—but so will yours. A little bird told me that the authorities on Lemnos have not been cooperating. They don't like your investigation! I'd be surprised if your shuttle full of Security Guardians is in a great hurry to get here. Or whether they'll get here at all. I don't play chess, Sousanna, but I know the game. I'm not in check; *you* are."

"Then it's just you and me?"

"I think we have a stalemate, my dear. How about calling it a tie? You don't have proof of anything, and you don't really want a messy shootout, do you? You have a distinguished future career to think about, just as I do. So: you leave, and you send a message to tell your Guardian friends that they're not needed. They won't mind that! I stay here, and help my friends to pack up."

"And what then?"

"Oh, I know you have some questions; and I might just have some answers. I won't be hiding. We'll meet again soon enough—I actually look forward to it!" She paused. "Come on, be fair: you gave *them* that option. You can have *my* solemn promise, too. Alright?"

"Alright."

They both lowered their tasers.

But Burk and Milliya were already many leagues away, speeding—as fast as Milliya could push the shuttle, which was not, after all, a racing vessel— towards Lemnos City.

CHAPTER THIRTEEN
WATCH ME BECOME
A NEW PERSON

FOR A LONG TIME Burk didn't say anything. He just gazed gloomily out at the Northern Lemnian Plain. Nor did he cheer up when Milliya told him that their timing was perfect, and that they could catch the *Starspringer* at the Gate of Lemnos if they got to Lemnos City that evening without mishap. Jacoob had promised that someone would meet them. Someone would get them onboard.

"So what? We'll just be arrested back on Terra, or on the ship, and not here on Lemnos. What difference does that make?"

Milliya asked him whether he had packed away the soil samples.

"Yes, but what do they prove? They could be anything, from anywhere on Lemnos. We need the recording that you made on your communicator! And now Guardian Rebek'a has it. She'll delete it the first chance she gets. But the fake stuff—she won't delete *that*, she'll show it to everyone."

"And you don't think that Guardian Sousanna will

confiscate it from her?" Milliya suggested. And for some reason, she smiled.

Burk didn't think that it was likely to happen.

"Why should she do that? She's outranked. And she was more interested in arresting *us* than investigating anyone else. Rebek'a will copy it for her, and delete the rest, or throw the communicator away."

"No, I don't think so. She hasn't got the recordings."

"I saw you throw her the communicator!"

"No you didn't." Once again she smiled at him, very sweetly, as she often did when she was pointing out something stupid he had done. "Burk: do you *always* believe what you see? If you do, we can forget trying to get you into the Guardians!"

"But I saw you throw it!"

"So you saw me throw...*this*?" And she reached inside her top and fetched out a personal communicator. "This is my communicator. Everything that we need is on here. Proof of who the Outsiders are. Proof that the settlers have been up to no good. Okay, we haven't seen them cutting down *sqot*, and we don't know exactly what they've been up to, but those samples may help. And as for what you call the fake stuff: put that together with our recording, and any objective judge will see a cover-up."

She passed the communicator to Burk, who looked at it sceptically.

"Are you sure this is yours?"

Except for cruder planetary models like the one that Leyna had used, all personal communicators looked very much the same until you switched them on, unless you were prepared to peer at the tiny personal code number on the base.

"I'm sure that it's mine."

"So what was it that you threw across to Rebek'a?"

"That was Aylwin's communicator. I just happened to have it with me."

"Why?"

"Oh, I was watching the recordings on it while you were busy doing other things. For the most part, home-made entertainment material, rather in the style of Gloriya's movie highlights, but more *explicit*. Aylwin is always the star. You see him performing heroic deeds in a number of different situations...and positions. It wasn't intended for a mainstream audience, I would say—it's a bit *too* unorthodox. If Guardian Rebek'a is now looking at the recordings, as I suspect she might be, she'll be impressed by the technical quality. Not by the content, though!"

"And you didn't share it with me?"

"No, I censored it. You're only an innocent little AdPop, and you need to be protected from images like that. Don't look so disappointed! We still have Keesha's communicator—who knows what that might contain!"

But they didn't switch it on. Keesha and Aylwin might have been found, and someone could already be tracking the missing communicators.

They reached Lemnos City at dusk and went straight to the spaceport. They had been hoping to be able to lose themselves in the great crush of travelers and their friends and relatives, but most of the incomings who had disembarked from the *Starspringer* had already been processed, and there were comparatively few passengers waiting to be embarked onto the transit shuttles.

Discouragingly, there were Guardians everywhere they looked. And there was no sign of Jacoob. Security, identity and customs procedures were reportedly more time-consuming for passengers leaving Lemnos than for those arriving, if only because the staff had more time for them. Burk and Milliya were Wanted Persons. They had packed carefully—except for Milliya's personal communicator, their bags contained nothing that in a routine search would identify them as who they really were, or even as "Guardian Jo-anna" and "Markko Mann"—but there was no way that they'd be able to embark without completely new identities. They needed new documents, and something had to be done about the data on their identity chips.

They went over to stand in front of the DELICIO DELIGHTS restaurant, which was predictably half empty. Jacoob would be able to spot them there more easily. Within minutes something indeed happened, though not what they had been hoping for. Two Grade I Guardians, their rank revealed by the single red slash on the shoulder of the uniform, marched over to Burk and Milliya and trained their tasers on them.

"Take your bags and come with us. We know who you are. Don't do anything silly!"

In a state of shock, Burk found Milliya and himself

being marched out of the main concourse, down a side passageway and into what appeared to be a set of unoccupied offices. The two Guardians pointed to a heavy door,

"In there!"

The room was dirty and windowless. It smelt unpleasant. There were tables and chairs, a number of small electronic items, and a large, ominous-looking piece of apparatus with electrodes, straps and footholds. This must be a room for interrogations. They were told to strip.

"We'll do you first, Guardian Milliya, if we may. Stand there, and we'll strap you in."

Surely the thing was too cumbersome and elaborate to be just for giving electric shocks? It had to be for some purpose more complex, more sinister, than that. Burk was surprised that the two Grade Is were going ahead without Guardian Rebek'a. She knew what they had, she would have realized that they would be making a run for it, and she must have overpowered her Guardian colleague and used her communicator, or Aylwin's, to contact her friends at the spaceport. It couldn't have been Guardian Sousanna—she would be expecting them to go into hiding on Lemnos, and she would have ordered them arrested, but not tortured.

The smaller of the two Guardians tied the straps around Milliya's wrists and ankles and then began attaching electrodes to her skin, including several close to her breasts. She grinned: "I hope this doesn't hurt. We don't get to do this very often."

Oh no, Burk thought, her breasts are so sensitive, this will be awful. And they're going to make me watch! Milliya herself looked surprisingly unfazed by what they were doing to her. Of course: she's been in torture cells like these before. She knows what's coming. She's placed the electrodes herself, and turned the dial. She's also had anti-torture training. Mind and body control. Breathing exercises. But will that help...?

"Stop!" he said. "This isn't necessary!"

"Yes it is, Mr. Burk."

"Please! We'll tell you what you want to know. Everything. You don't have to hurt her."

Both Guardians laughed. *And so did Milliya.*

"Burk, you are *pathetic*! I can't take you *anywhere*!"

"Mr. Burk," the taller of the two Guardians said, "don't you recognize me?"

He had been so preoccupied with his terror that Burk hadn't looked at the Guardians too closely.

"Burk, this is Guardian Abi. Surely you remember?"

"Slabface" from the *Starstretcher*!

"Pleased to see you again, Mr. Burk. My, you're nervous. Would it help if we shook hands?"

Burk was thoroughly ashamed of himself. But shaking hands, first with Guardian Abi and then with her colleague, who was introduced as Guardian Toyah, did help to calm him. Among other things, it was a rare honor for a Guardian to offer her hand to an AdPop.

"Jacoob couldn't come. Toyah is his sister."

Burk couldn't see any family resemblance.

"I share many of his political views, Mr. Burk, but

I can do more good *inside* the organization than from the outside. My brother didn't have that choice. He's a very clever man, but the Guardians don't take hunchbacks."

"And Guardian Abi?"

"He's my boyfriend, Mr. Burk. You know how we Guardian girls like to exploit innocent AdPops!"

"I don't know why I bother with this one, though. Burk, you are such an idiot! Did you really think they were going to torture us? Abi, come on, let's put a few electrodes on him just to teach him a lesson!"

But there was no time for that. The purpose of the machinery was to alter their basic identity chips. On the journey out to Lemnos, the problem had been solved by using proxy identities for disembarkation. These were programmed into the scanners on the *Starstretcher* to override whatever information was actually on their implants. And they had sent this false information through the wire to the scanners at the Gate.

The checks during embarkation might be more rigorous, though; it would be tricky manipulating the system on the *Starspringer* at such short notice—they hadn't known until a few minutes before that Burk and Milliya would be traveling on that date, and on that ship—and it would be impossible to trick the identity and security controls back on Terra. So, for better or for worse, they would need new identities for the whole journey.

"Watch me become a new person, Burk!"

Guardian Toyah had brought the files on her

personal communicator, which was plugged in to the machine. They were transferred through the electrodes to Milliya's identity chip. She shuddered several times while this was happening—was it a sort of torture after all?—and it was explained to Burk that these quite harmless reactions sometimes caused the electrodes to shift or fall off, hence the need for straps. He was very apprehensive, but when his turn came he felt no pain, only an uncomfortable tingling sensation.

Milliya was now UsePop Miley; Burk was now her husband Mytt.

"We've based the profiles on typical settler biographies. You are now UsePops. Mr. Burk has therefore been promoted. Abi has put all the details on Milliya's communicator, and deleted the real personal information. You're going to like your new personalities!"

Burk thought of Gloriya and Jonn, Keesha and Aylwin, and assumed that Guardian Toyah was being ironic.

"And there is one big advantage, of course—you get to share a cabin on the *Starspringer*! Now, let's hurry."

For passengers leaving for Terra, the main customs control was at the spaceport, not at the Gate: that way, if anything illicit was found, the passenger didn't have to be carted back to Lemnos on a shuttle. Would there be a search of their luggage? What if someone found the samples of soil? They didn't look like Lemnian crystals or colored dust. But their bags were light. So as not to arouse suspicion at the estate, they had packed them to look like what you would typically take on a short "safari". They had deliberately left most of their clothes behind, but they could buy additional clothes on the *Starspringer*, and Abi told them that this would be a fast trip to Terra, with a lot of time spent in transportation pods while the ship was in high slide. In the event, nobody asked them to open up their bags.

On the transit shuttle, they had a bay to themselves. No settlers came and pestered them. *They* were the settlers now. They would have to live up to their new identities, practice being smug, selfish and materialistic, behave convincingly like people who in their spare time ate *sqot* and went to orgies. On board the *Starspringer*, they must be Miley and Mytt. Guardian Rebek'a would be looking everywhere for them. She might have some contacts on the ship. Those people would have instructions to kill them and destroy their evidence.

"And that's only the beginning, darling. What do we do when we get back to Terra? The most powerful people in the universe are going to be interested in us: what we found out, what we know. Can we play that game, Burk? I'm only a Grade I!"

She looked down at the planet they were leaving. The surface seemed to be glowing dark red—not dark-green, as it was claimed in so many tourists' accounts, and not the arid gray-brown that most new arrivals witnessed. *It's sending me a message, she thought.*

"I feel that we owe something to Lemnos. That there's a debt that needs to be paid."

At the Gate, there was no Guardian Georgeena—it

must have been her day off. Just as well, because there was only one queue. It would have taken ages if she had been on duty.

APPENDIX
TERRAN SOCIAL STRATA

Guardian V—Senior leadership

Guardian IV—Junior leadership
  *G. Mykel (Commander of the *Starstretcher*)

Guardian III—Officers
  G. Rebek'a (Senior Level, Ideology)
  *G. Adriyan (Social and Recreational)
  *G. (retired) Silvia
  G. Sousanna (Crime and Security)

Guardian II—Non-commissioned officers
  *G. "Cruella"

Guardian I—Rank and file
  G. Abi ("Slabface")
  G. Georgeena
  G. Milliya
  G. Toyah

Useful population (UsePop)—Made up of "breeders" (f) and their "consorts" (m)
   Gloriya
   Keesha
   Aylwin (Keesha's husband)
   Gylberto
   Jonn (Gloriya's husband)

Additional population (AdPop)—Made up of "ladies" (f) and "drones" (m)
   Dhavid (crewman)
   John Burk
   Jacoob (scribe)

Surplus population (SurPop)—Underclass, convicts, criminals, addicts, social undesirables
   Leyna

   * = Appears only in *The Gate of Lemnos*.

ABOUT THE AUTHOR

FRANCIS JARMAN was born in Germany but brought up and educated in England. According to family tradition, he is descended from the Thracian slave Androcles (of *Androcles and the Lion* fame). Dr. Jarman teaches comparative cultural studies and intercultural communication at the University of Hildesheim (Germany), but has also taught or lectured in Belgium, Bulgaria, Cyprus, Denmark, Egypt, England, Finland, Greece, India, Italy, Japan, Lithuania, Malta, Poland, Portugal, Spain, and Thailand. A playwright, novelist, and classical numismatist, he has on his travels met a goddess, danced in public with eunuchs, stroked a lion, sat on a snake, encountered sacred rats, and been attacked by a pig, arrested by a military patrol, and involved in the hold-up of a train by bandits (though none of these events have appeared so far in his fiction).